CHAINS

JON RICHTER

www.bloodhoundbooks.com

Print ISBN 978-1-5040-7782-8

ALSO BY JON RICHTER

Never Rest

———

Rabbit Hole

———

The Warden

For my father. I might often disagree with you, but I'll always appreciate your encouragement.

URSULA PEMBRIDGE

(DETECTIVE SERGEANT, CHESHIRE CONSTABULARY)

The sign was partially obscured by the trees. Their wind-jostled branches seemed to paw at it, like beggars clawing at some wealthy traveller who'd appeared in their midst. Ursula almost missed the side road, but managed to slow the unmarked car in time, her headlights illuminating the autumn-cloaked foliage as she proceeded along the driveway. Dead leaves squelched under her tyres.

Brookhaven Hall
A Harrington and Braithwaite Care Home

She had never been to the former stately home – once a crumbling nest of squatters and drug users, now an upmarket retirement facility – because her police officer's salary wasn't enough to afford somewhere like this for her own poor, dementia-suffering mum. *At least I visit her regularly*, she thought as the manor loomed ahead of her, *instead of shoving her out here in some luxurious oubliette.* She knew this was a bitter, fruitless line of thinking, as was dwelling on the paltry pay increases with which the government had seen fit to furnish her over the past decade, or the austerity measures that were partly to blame for her being here alone, preparing to secure the scene before the Scenes Of Crime Officers started work at 7am. These days they only had one SOCO on call overnight, and he hadn't bloody answered.

No point complaining about that now, of course; she'd have to wait for the upcoming General Election to have her say about the budget cuts. For now, she needed to concentrate on the job in hand. She still wasn't entirely sure what she expected to find; usually when the elderly died at a place like this, only a doctor would attend, to formally declare the death before the undertaker collected the corpse. *It will be mum one day*, she realised with a shiver. *And one day it will be you too, if some drug dealer doesn't cave your head in before you've even had a chance to see Hayley finish growing up.*

She forced her train of thought away from that desolate track and back to the matter at hand. A doctor would attend when no foul play was involved, but Ursula was there because of the two emergency calls the police had received. The first call, from one of the staff at the care home, had provided a garbled and hysterical account of a stabbing and a fatality. The second had come soon afterwards; an anonymous call apparently from a different person, calmly stating that someone had been killed at the old folks' home and hanging up before the call handler could ask any further questions. Something odd was definitely going on. As the officer on call at five thirty in the morning, Ursula had been asked to investigate.

A thin mist of ice-cold rain nibbled gleefully at her as she clambered out of the car, and she shielded her face as she negotiated her way from the car park to the building's front entrance. The surrounding trees seemed to watch her from a distance, whispering to each other. *Who's she? What's happened?* The door was locked, so she found and pressed the nearby intercom buzzer. A hesitant female voice told her to wait, that she'd be right down. Ursula leaned forwards to peer through the window. Through it, she saw a spacious hallway with a wide staircase that curved around as it led upwards.

A couple of old people, male and female, were shuffling around the base of the stairs, and she couldn't help but think of the zombies in the TV series she'd been binge-watching between shifts. She shuddered again, watching their slow, shambling movements. They looked like bad animatronics, like B-movie parodies of the people they'd been before. When the door opened, she half expected to hear them moaning insistently for *brainnnsss*.

A uniformed blonde girl appeared on the staircase, hurrying down towards her. She was one of those people whose petite build and elfin features meant she would probably always look about eighteen years old, at least from a distance. As Ursula approached, she could see the girl's cheeks were streaked with tears, and that her pretty eyes were wide and haunted. The sockets seemed to be receding from the eyeballs, like diseased gums from bad teeth. 'Are you the police?' the girl asked as she opened the door. Her voice had a desperate, frightened edge to it.

'I am. Detectives don't wear a uniform.' Ursula flashed her warrant card. 'May I come in?'

'Oh, thank you, thank you,' the girl mumbled. 'I'm so glad you're here.'

She moved to one side, and Ursula stepped across the threshold, glad to be out of the rain. The acrid tang of pine cleaner assaulted her nostrils, but couldn't entirely mask the converted mansion's underlying odour, which was ancient and earthy, inhabiting the air like a ghostly presence. The effect was of a long-buried crypt given a hasty spring-clean. 'I'm Detective

Sergeant Pembridge,' Ursula said. 'Was it you who made the call?'

'Yes. He's this way.' Before Ursula could ask any further questions, the girl turned and hurried back towards the staircase, opening the gate that was presumably there to prevent the oldies from attempting to climb it. *Imagine being banned from going upstairs*, Ursula thought. It's as if they've regressed to being little children.

A cruel, inevitable cycle.

She glanced down at the two old people as they ascended. The old woman had stumbled off down an adjoining passage, but the man was still there, staring at Ursula with a sad glimmer of mistaken recognition in his eyes. 'Are you the only staff member working tonight?' Ursula asked, trying to ignore him. The old man continued to watch her, his face full of confused yearning, toothless lips straining to form a question. Ursula was glad they quickly made it out of earshot.

'There's one other. Supposed to be three of us, but someone rang in sick.'

'Only two on duty, in a place this size?'

The girl didn't reply. She just kept climbing, almost running, in fact. Ursula realised she was desperate to share whatever horrors awaited them upstairs. To unburden herself.

'What's your name?' Ursula persisted as they reached the first floor landing and she was led down a long, tiled corridor.

'Stephanie,' replied the woman. 'Stephanie Glebe.' Her guide's voice trembled and threatened to break as she spoke, and Ursula realised Stephanie was holding back tears.

'Can you tell me what's happened, Stephanie?' she pressed gently. 'They told me one of the old people had died.'

Stephanie stopped, turning to her with a look of dismay. 'It's not a *resident*! Don't they bloody *listen* when people ring 999?' She pointed towards a doorway a few metres further along, remaining rooted to the spot as though she couldn't bear to get any closer to the room beyond. 'Please... he's in there.'

I can ask her more questions later, Ursula thought. *First, let's see what we're dealing with here.* She approached the door, an old oak slab with a plastic sign attached to it saying 'office'. It stood ajar, so she eased it open with her foot. The sign was accurate: the room was indeed an office, housing a desk faced by two high-backed chairs, various filing cabinets, and shelves piled with documents. There were pot plants and ornamental vases, and a large portrait on the left-hand wall of some long-dead aristocrat, sneering as he surveyed the scene. Opposite her was a large window, spattered on the outside by the rain.

On the inside, the window was smeared with a long, bloody handprint. The bright fingermarks arced downwards to where a man was slouched in a chair. The seat was tilted slightly away from the desk, the man staring up at the ceiling as if he was taking a momentary break from his work.

Ursula rushed towards him, but even as she rounded the desk, she was immediately certain he was dead. A huge volume of blood had gushed from a wound in his left abdomen, soaking his once-white shirt and navy trousers and creating a spreading Rorschach blotch on the beige carpet. His mouth hung slackly beneath his wide eyes, right hand still clutching his belly as though he thought hiding the injury from view might make it magically disappear. His other hand reached out to rest on the desk as if he'd been determined to sign the papers that were spread out there, but had managed in the end to leave only another grisly red smudge.

The deceased man was old, his hair entirely grey; his jowly face was lined and slightly jaundiced in hue. Yet his smart attire, clean-shaven cheeks, and his location in this office suggested that Stephanie had been right: this was not a resident. Ursula had no time to ponder his identity any further, because an old lady in a nightdress was squatting close to the desk, rummaging in the wastepaper basket.

'Where is it? Why do they always hide our things, Robbie? You'll tell them, won't you? You'll take them all to court, these swine, these rotten buggers...' The woman's cantankerous muttering continued as she tossed scraps of paper, Post-it notes and empty water bottles into the air, searching frantically for some fragment of her ruined memory.

'Stephanie! I need you in here now, please.' Ursula hoped she'd projected enough authority into her voice to override the care worker's fear of entering the room. Trying to ignore the old woman, Ursula attended to the seated figure and checked his pulse; as she expected, there was no heartbeat. But judging by his temperature, he hadn't been dead long.

Stephanie appeared in the doorway, averting her eyes from the body. 'Mrs Vickers!' she cried. 'You know you're not supposed to be in here!'

The old lady stood up, emptying the bin's remaining contents all over the floor with an exasperated grunt. 'It's not here!' she grumbled. 'What will Robbie say? He'll be home from work soon, and he'll want his tea...'

Behind her, the sour-faced aristocrat in the painting continued to smirk. *So much for securing the crime scene, Sergeant.*

'Shhh, Mrs Vickers,' said Stephanie, steering the old woman gently towards the door. 'Come with me, and we'll go and find Robbie together.'

'Get your colleague, and come back as soon as you can,' Ursula instructed the care worker. 'I need them to make sure no one else gets in here until more officers arrive, so you and I can go somewhere to talk more about what happened.'

'Okay,' Stephanie replied glumly. Her expression suggested

she'd prefer to do literally anything else, including listening to Mrs Vickers' ongoing monologue.

'Who is he, by the way?' Ursula asked, glancing again at the body in the chair. 'I feel like I recognise him.'

Stephanie ushered the old woman into the hallway, then turned, her expression seeming to encompass too many emotions. 'It's John Harrington,' she sniffed.

A Harrington and Braithwaite Care Home.

Of course. Ursula knew the local tycoon from his incessant local public appearances. John Harrington was a master of self-promotion, often seen appearing at award shows or other ceremonies, shaking hands and handing over gigantic charity cheques. Unlike his reclusive business partner, Harrington was happy to attend the opening of an envelope, as long as he could be photographed alongside it.

Ursula frowned. Why would the multi-millionaire co-owner of a successful property group be at work overnight in one of his own retirement homes? More importantly, why had someone killed him? And *who*?

The buzz of the intercom sliced through Ursula's musings, making her jump. Thankfully Stephanie had already turned away, and didn't witness her microsecond of weakness. Neither did John Harrington, because he would never witness anything, ever again.

Only the aristocrat in the painting saw it, and appeared greatly amused.

'Whoever it is, tell them they can't come up here,' Ursula called after Stephanie. But minutes later, they did exactly that, Stephanie reappearing in the doorway along with a bland-looking, suited man. He looked confused and worried, as well as middle-aged, middle-sized and thoroughly unremarkable.

'What's going on?' he asked, wiping sleep from his eyes, blinking at the corpse like a man who thought he might be hallucinating.

'You can't come in here, sir,' Ursula replied with an irritated sigh, striding forwards to block his view.

'But I'm Eric Potter's campaign lead,' the man replied anxiously. 'He's due to visit this place in less than two hours!'

2

OWEN CAULFIELD

(SENIOR CONSTITUENCY ASSISTANT TO ERIC POTTER MP)

Owen hung up, and massaged the bridge of his nose with his free hand.

'Did he answer?' asked Brian, from the room's opposite corner. Owen looked at him, realising he couldn't remember the last time he'd seen his dad out of that armchair. It was as if its grotesque floral pattern had grown around him, intertwining with his old bones like some hideous symbiote.

'Nope. I just left a message. I should probably leave another with Shelley in case he doesn't pick it up.'

Brian sneered. 'Probably still in bed, the lazy bastard.'

'It *is* only seven thirty.'

'See, that's the whole problem nowadays – no one has any standards. You young people–'

'I'm thirty-nine, Dad,' Owen interjected, to no avail.

'–can't be bothered to roll out of bed until after nine, and now neither can your politicians.'

'What, and you think Nigel Hawke is different?' he scoffed. 'The Tories are all hopping out from under their eiderdowns at half six every day?'

'Hawke is the best of a bad bunch.'

Owen pinched the bridge of his nose again, drawing in what he intended to be a long, cleansing breath. Instead, he inhaled a lungful of the dusty, sweaty odour of his dad's room, which only made him angrier. The old man sat there, dispensing his misguided lectures, while he couldn't even be bothered to maintain decent standards of personal hygiene.

'Look, I know you aren't a fan of Eric,' Owen said acidly. 'I'm not either, and I bloody work for him. But how a man like you, who claims to be some sort of working-class hero...' Here Owen gestured at the ridiculous assemblage of nationalist paraphernalia – everything from the obligatory massive England flag to display cases of various coins and medals, old ration books, even an authentic World War One helmet – that was crammed onto the walls of his father's modest room. '...Someone who never tires of reminding me that my granddad fought Hitler only to die "down t'pit", and that *his* dad died in the trenches in the First World War; how you can vote Conservative is utterly beyond me! I'd have thought you'd be the last person to swallow a load of Tory propaganda.'

He knew he shouldn't get angry. His dad was old, and stubborn, and preyed upon by the unscrupulous right wing and its obedient press. Dominic Cummings probably had photos of men like him pinned to a whiteboard with 'key demographic' written underneath. Maybe with a laughing emoji scrawled alongside.

'Look, I'm not an idiot,' Brian snapped. 'I don't even really care about politics. I just want people to treat each other properly, like in the good old days.'

'That's exactly the problem! They've got you all harking back to some imaginary yesteryear when everyone lived in a little quaint Postman Pat village, and all the nasty foreigners weren't allowed in to spoil it. The world's moving on, Dad.'

'Who said anything about foreigners? I'm not racist!'

'But that's what this election is really about!' Owen couldn't help himself. 'The government have convinced the public that everything will magically get better overnight as soon as they "get Brexit done". I mean, we live in bloody Axton, for God's sake! It's overwhelmingly white, even for the north-west. Yet somehow they've got everyone scapegoating immigrants for all their problems. *Paid a pittance? Blame Brussels! Can't get a job? A foreigner probably nicked it!*'

'All right, all right, I get your point. We'll have to agree to disagree.'

Owen expelled an infuriated sigh, placing his phone down on the arm of his chair so he could upgrade from nose-bridge-squeeze to full head-in-hands exasperation. 'At least you don't have to worry about Eric coming here in person today anymore,' he said eventually. 'Not now it's a bloody crime scene.'

When the girl had answered the door in tears and directed him upstairs to speak to the policewoman, Owen had thought for a horrible moment that something had happened to his dad. An irrational assumption; and one that proved, much to his annoyance, that he must still care about the misguided old curmudgeon, somewhere deep down.

Instead, he'd been confronted by a corpse. The image still chilled him. It had been like a waxwork, like a plastic dummy set up in a theme park haunted house ride.

Brian chuckled darkly. 'It's a good job you did get here early to check on the place – imagine if Potter *had* turned up, with reporters and everything, only to find out John Harrington's dead body was upstairs! You could have had it in the papers: *MP so slimy that local businessman tops himself to avoid meeting him.*'

Owen fought very hard not to smile at the quip. 'Is that what's happened? He committed suicide?'

His dad shrugged. 'You saw him, so you know more than

me. They haven't bloody told us anything. Only that there's been an accident, and the whole west wing is sealed off. I only know it's Harrington 'cos Stephanie told me.'

'Stephanie?'

'The nice blonde one who looks after me.'

Owen felt a pang of guilt, realising he'd paid almost no attention to the Brookhaven staff, even the one that had escorted him to his dad's room after his long and frustrating conversation with the detective.

'I don't really know what the point of him visiting here was in the first place,' the old man continued, light-hearted tone quickly evaporating. Owen scowled; he'd already told his father that Potter's latest public appearance was his own idea, which meant that the comment was presumably intended as a criticism, as were most of the remarks Brian aimed in his direction.

'It was meant to be a two-birds-one-stone type of thing,' he replied evenly, trying to control the temper he knew he'd inherited from the stocky, stubble-chinned man sitting opposite. 'I wanted to show that Eric's in touch with normal people in the community, but also that he's supportive of big business, like Harrington and Braithwaite.'

Now just Braithwaite. The thought, like the body he'd glimpsed, had a surreal quality, utterly alien and out of place in an otherwise typical, rain-sodden November morning.

'Big business.' Brian snorted. 'I could have been a rich man too, if my bloody family had supported me.'

And there it was. A perfectly pleasant, or at least largely civil, conversation ruined by a deftly-deployed verbal hand grenade. Owen had no doubt that his dad did it on purpose: it was like an open wound Brian couldn't help but jam his index finger into. He already knew the well-travelled downward spiral their conversation would now inevitably follow: his dad blaming his mother for abandoning him and his glazing company, as though the bankruptcy was anything other than completely inevitable given his dad's appalling business decisions; his dad blaming Owen and his sister for not disowning their mother after her affair; his dad blaming bank managers and the government for denying him the loans and support he felt he was entitled to.

Owen had neither the energy for it, nor the energy to avoid it. 'Maybe you shouldn't have gotten into so much debt,' he heard himself saying.

Mercifully, even as some caustic response was forming on Brian's lips, there was a knock at the door. It opened to reveal a young, fair-haired care worker, the 'nice blonde one' his dad had been referring to earlier.

'I'm sorry to disturb you both,' she said. 'Just letting Brian know that breakfast is still on, but it's going to be a bit delayed.'

'Oh, thanks, love,' replied Brian. 'Aren't they letting you off shift yet, after the night you've had?' Owen found himself resenting the warmth in his father's tone. Always such kindness for complete strangers, but never for his own wife or children. Why did he think Mum had left him, and that Owen's sister didn't even bother to visit?

Then again, in this case, this woman was not a stranger at all, but someone Brian presumably saw regularly. In fact, the old man might be closer to this girl than anyone in his own family. What a peculiar situation, his father's life here. Despite being in possession of a full set of marbles and not yet too badly deteriorated in his mobility, Brian had actually seemed quite keen to relocate to Brookhaven when Owen had suggested it. It was partly financially motivated; his dad's landlord had decided to sell the little bungalow that had been Brian's home since the divorce, and the dilapidated house's rent had been low even for

Axton, meaning it was difficult for the old man to find a suitable new place.

And maybe Brian also liked the promise of company. Owen didn't exactly visit the old man very often, either.

'Soon,' the girl replied. 'The copper just wants to ask me some more questions.'

'Well I'm sure you'll be all right... as long as you didn't kill him, eh?'

He winked, making Owen cringe. The woman visibly blanched, but still managed to force a polite laugh. Jesus, what a life: when she wasn't cleaning up old people's shit, she was having to listen to it. Owen watched the door close behind her.

'Lovely lass, that one,' Brian reiterated. 'Needs someone to look after her, though – her husband sounds like a useless twerp.'

Owen looked at his father, and at the patriotic bric-a-brac that surrounded him. A seventy-eight-year-old man with a mind as cluttered as the single room that had become his home; a jumble of muddled ideologies and misplaced chivalry. Owen had no children of his own yet. He wondered if he would one day sit opposite a son or daughter of his own, in a room like this. If he did, would he detect in their gaze the same toxic mixture of pity, guilt and revulsion he now felt?

His phone rang, giving him an excuse to leave. He saw *Eric Potter* on the display, and held up a hand in a half-hearted apology as he rose from his chair, heading out into the corridor to take the call.

3

STEPHANIE GLEBE

(CARE WORKER, BROOKHAVEN HALL)

The copper had a *lot* more questions for her, it turned out. Once the day shift had started, Stephanie didn't have any excuse not to submit to DS Pembridge's interrogation. Sitting forlornly in the dining area the detective had temporarily converted into a makeshift interview room, she'd been grilled like one of Brookhaven's soggy breakfast tomatoes. Now her brain felt exhausted, barely functioning at all, a machine running on an emergency backup generator. She yearned for sleep to bring blissful shutdown, temporary nothingness, and had to concentrate on keeping her eyes open as she drove back towards town. Soon after she passed the neglected scar of the old mine, where her granddad had once worked, the trees gradually began to thin out, signalling the end of Brookhaven's rural setting.

Before long, Stephanie was driving through the familiar, dismal wasteland of Axton town centre. Miserable buildings sagged in long rows alongside the main street as if they'd been fly-tipped there: kebab shops with their shutters down, newsagents with indecipherable names, grotty upstairs flats with weeds growing out of cracks around the window frames. A place she hated, but could never escape from. She felt like a child, like Harry Potter locked in his auntie's cupboard under the stairs.

But you're not *a child anymore, Stephanie; you have a husband and a kid of your own, and neither of them know how to make breakfast or lunch. You've got four missed calls from Dan already, which probably means Nicky went to school without any food – if he's even gone to school at all.*

And it will all be your fault for being late.

She knew it wouldn't be long before she arrived home – at this hour she had a chance of finding a parking space somewhere near the front door, because all the other cars would have been driven to work by now, at least those whose owners had jobs to go to – and forced herself to push those concerns from her mind, to savour a few more minutes of peace. But her brain was only filled immediately by other worries, and she found herself reflecting again on her 'chat' with the policewoman, who had been friendly but firm, patient but insistent.

Stephanie had told the copper that she'd found the body slumped in its chair when she went in to offer Harrington a cup of tea at about four thirty in the morning, and had called the police straight away. No, she didn't know why he was working there overnight. Indeed, it was very unusual for him to visit the home at all; it probably had something to do with the MP's planned visit, which she imagined was now cancelled. She didn't know much about politics, nor care. As far as she was concerned, they were all as bad as each other; liars and creeps and perverts. She did know that the MP, Porter or whatever his name was, visited the Cabin from time to time, but that wasn't information she felt she needed to share with the police.

She also hadn't told the copper that, only a few hours before his death, she'd given oral sex to Harrington in the same room he had died in.

How could she? It had been made very clear to her that the Cabin, and anything relating to Harrington's 'other' business interests, were to be kept completely secret, with severe consequences for anyone who blabbed about them. Besides, that sideline was her business, an alternative career in which the money came in cash, without tax or NI deductions. At least it meant she could keep some for herself.

She smiled grimly. Part of her was disgusted at the thought of the crumpled twenty-pound notes in her purse, but part of her had almost felt honoured when Harrington had asked her; normally she was pleasuring his business associates or sleazy friends out at the Cabin, not the boss himself. At least his death meant she was unlikely to get called upon today, and so wouldn't have to think up some excuse for Dan about an emergency babysitting job or a night shift that needed to be covered at short notice. Every lie she told to her husband felt like a bruise on her heart, although to be honest, she wasn't sure he would even care. As long as her money kept rolling in, helping him with his gambling or Bitcoin or whatever new scam he'd been swept up in, he was happy.

Perhaps she shouldn't be so hard on him. At least he never hit her, unlike some of her friends' husbands and boyfriends.

A prostitute and a penniless gambling addict; but hey, at least he doesn't beat you up. What a fairy-tale marriage.

She turned onto her estate, noticing some fresh graffiti on the side of her neighbour's garage. Someone had daubed a grinning face with two huge eyes, and the image immediately brought back another memory from the previous night, one that made her blood turn to crushed ice. Should she have told the copper about the monster she'd seen, out there amongst the trees? No, because she would have sounded completely insane.

It was when the rain had been really bucketing down, after the blow job but before she'd found John's body. There'd been rumblings of thunder, a few flickers of half-hearted lightning. Stephanie had been downstairs, staring out of the back door into the woods, sipping tea while she listened for any ominous noises from the old duffers, whose capacity to injure themselves never ceased to amaze her. There'd been a sudden flash, blue-white and startling, illuminating the trees so clearly she'd thought she could discern their different shades of yellow and brown, reminding her of elderly people's piss and shit. In that fraction of a second, something else had caught her eye; or at least that's what her brain believed, after the darkness returned and all she had was an after-image, fading and already dreamlike, underscored by the growl of sluggish thunder.

A figure, staring back at her through giant black eyeballs. It had looked like an alien, like a creature from *The X-Files*. It was standing amongst the trees, unmoving, impossible. And terrifying.

You just need some sleep, Stephanie. And to hide the cash from Dan before he fritters it away.

When Stephanie arrived home, her husband was waiting for her at the front door, looking angry.

4

DANIEL GLEBE

(CONSTRUCTION OPERATIVE, HARRINGTON AND BRAITHWAITE PROPERTY GROUP)

'It's like she does it on purpose, Bruno, you know? To undermine me.'

'Does what? Works late?'

Dan screwed up his face. 'No, not that! If she gets paid overtime for it, good – we need the money anyway. I mean ignoring my calls, like I'm not as important as her precious bloody job. I bet your missus isn't selfish like that?'

His work colleague shifted his eyes momentarily from the road to glance at him. Bruno's spliff hung out of the open car window, at the end of the thick slab of his left arm, but his breath still brought some of the weed stink with it. Dan grimaced. He wasn't into that stuff. Bruno was lucky they worked on a site that didn't bother with random drug testing.

'Selfish? At least your wife work. Mine sit at home all day, miserable.'

'That's because you've got four kids, Bruno. Didn't they sell johnnies back in Latvia?'

'All my children are born in UK. I live here for years, asshole.'

Dan laughed, punching his co-worker in the shoulder. Co-worker, not friend, never friend. People always stabbed you in the back eventually, so Dan had long ago decided it was better not to let your guard down. 'Only joking, Bruno. Now put your foot down a bit; Jesus, you drive like my nan.'

'Maybe you should learn drive yourself.'

It was only a bit of banter, but Dan found himself stung by the comment. He wondered if people laughed at him, a man whose wife could drive a car while he relied on lifts to get himself to work. He'd even had to go round to a neighbour's that morning, cap in hand, asking if they could take Nicky to school because Steph hadn't come home in time.

He fell silent as Bruno continued along the grubby streets, past the industrial estate, towards the patch of barren wasteland where they both worked. He glanced at the sign as Bruno turned onto the site, cheered up by the sight of the bird shit that was still smeared across the first word, making it look like a crude pun. Dan had pointed it out to people, but no one seemed to find it as funny as he did. Boring bastards.

Coming soon
A Harrington and Braithwaite development

He sneered. The sign made it sound like they were building something grand and exclusive, not the generic, cut-every-corner, high-rise cuboid he was there to help assemble. Sometimes he wondered if the people who bought or rented these places knew they were paying way over the odds for shoddy work. Sometimes he wondered if Harrington and Braithwaite didn't realise how shit their product was, or if they just didn't care.

He'd never seen Braithwaite – apparently the man was a bit of a hermit, and never visited the sites at all – but Harrington had sometimes turned up to rant and rave about slow progress, threatening to dock pay or sack everybody. At least that wasn't something Dan had to worry about anymore, not after the bombshell Steph had dropped on him that morning. The shock had taken the wind right out of the bollocking he'd been meaning to give her.

'I wonder if there's been anything on the radio?' he said. 'About Harrington carking it, I mean. Maybe no one else knows about it yet, and they'll have to announce it in the fucking health and safety briefings.'

Bruno nodded stoically, like some old soldier awaiting orders. For all Dan knew, maybe he once *had* been. To Dan, Bruno was one of those scary, formidable Eastern European types who looked like he'd survived a few wars. He was cagey about his past, describing himself as 'just an odd job man'. Dan didn't even really remember how they'd become acquaintances. A couple of blokes, working on a building site, trying to earn a living. He almost felt guilty about voting for Brexit, which probably meant Bruno would get deported or whatever.

They parked up and headed in to put on their PPE, and sure enough they were asked to assemble in the canteen rather than heading out to their usual work area. He'd never seen all the operatives in one place like this, all in matching high-vis overalls and hard hats, maybe fifty lads in total. Even the bosses were there: not only the site manager, but even the big dog herself, the project director. Yvette Morris sat in her wheelchair, surrounded by her cronies from the design team. In Dan's opinion, they were clueless plonkers who spent most of their time talking, constantly backtracking or changing the designs the construction team were supposed to build.

He even saw the jumped-up arsehole from head office, Harrington and Braithwaite's secretary or whatever he was. The Italian was wearing an immaculate suit, looking like he'd never done a day's hard graft in his life. Dan had had to show him around the site recently, and the sneering twerp had seemed more interested in keeping his shoes clean than looking at the half-built apartment block.

Dan nudged the oppo next to him, gesturing towards Morris as she moved forwards to address them. 'Look – it must be time for the Paralympics,' he whispered. The man glanced at him with an expression of disgust, and said nothing. Dan scowled. *Think you're too good to make jokes, do you? I'm better than all of you muppets. You'll see.*

'Good morning, everybody,' Yvette began. 'I'm afraid I have some very sad news for all of you.'

Dan glanced around smugly at the puzzled faces, smiling as he realised he was one of the only people with the inside scoop. It was the same as the Bitcoin: they'd all still be slaving away here while he was making a fortune from his smart investments.

Oh yeah? said the voice in his head, the voice he despised. *Like the fortune you made on the horses last weekend?*

It spoke in the voice of the hundred schoolkids who'd picked on him, a chorus of a thousand job applications that had responded 'thanks but no thanks'.

Your 10-1 'cert' fell at the first fence, you loser.

The voice of his dad, embarrassed when his son came home crying.

Humiliated that he'd fathered such a pathetic little wimp.

Dan's smile faded as the project director continued.

5

YVETTE MORRIS

(PROJECT DIRECTOR, HARRINGTON AND
BRAITHWAITE PROPERTY GROUP)

'Last night, John Harrington, one of our co-owners, passed away.'

Yvette surveyed the assembled faces. A few of them bore the sullen cast of underappreciated workers, pissed off at someone from upper management interfering in their day. It was an expression she was used to and an attitude she'd learned to deal with as she'd progressed rapidly up the ranks, despite working in such a male-dominated profession. Most, though, looked suitably shaken by the news. 'There are already some rumours doing the rounds, but we would like to ask people to please be respectful, and not to speculate on the specifics of what happened until we're able to share more information.'

She knew the specifics, or at least more than had been publicly announced. Yvette could scarcely believe what had happened herself. Their co-owner had been stabbed to death, in his office at Brookhaven Hall. She knew the details would inevitably leak out somehow, but Ian Braithwaite had been *very* insistent on their leadership team call that morning that they needed to keep a lid on things. Braithwaite had spoken to

23

Harrington's wife directly, and that was apparently the widow's wish, as well as the police's.

But can we trust Braithwaite? The thought had appeared in her mind as her boss had spoken, his voice an unsettling and sepulchral rasp. *What if he was involved in Harrington's death?* She knew it was a ridiculous idea. Yes, she was aware of the growing rift between the two businessmen, some big dispute relating to the company's finances and their failed bid to acquire the mine site. But the fact her bosses had been at each other's throats – the fact she'd rarely even met Braithwaite face to face despite working for him for five years, and found the reclusive and sinister little man much harder to deal with than his larger-than-life, now deceased business partner – was no reason to link him to a murder.

That's exactly how rumours start, Yvette. And you were told in no uncertain terms earlier that morning that your job is to quash them. She glanced at Giacomo, the executive assistant to Harrington and Braithwaite, whose darkly glittering gaze was fixed on her. *Sent here to keep an eye on me, no doubt.*

'Work will continue on site as normal,' she went on, mouth feeling suddenly dry. 'I know many of you work for sub-contractors, and that not every one of you has met Mr Harrington in person, but I know this news will still come as a shock. He was a good man and a fair employer, and he'll be sadly missed by his wife, his children, and his colleagues.'

There were a few cynical grumblings at this, but in the main the mood was silent and solemn, everyone as stunned as Yvette had felt when she'd first been informed of the killing less than an hour ago. She reflected on her words, wondering how many of them were true. Harrington had certainly always treated her fairly, although she'd hated his unannounced visits and despised his bad-tempered rants whenever she delivered bad news in her project review meetings. But she knew she should judge him by the experience she'd had of working for his company as an up-and-coming property developer.

Harrington had recruited her, a wheelchair user since the spinal injury she'd sustained in childhood, and made adjustments to accommodate her needs, even getting a lift installed out here on the construction site itself. She knew that was H and B's legal obligation, that she shouldn't think of it as some big favour; but she also knew that not every prospective employer would do so, especially up here in the north-west, where towns like Axton were hardly renowned for their inclusivity. Indeed, Harrington had been the one to personally offer Yvette her current job via a promotion, after the previous project director had left the company unexpectedly.

She thought about her predecessor. When he'd found out she'd be replacing him, Frank had sat her down and told her some other, far worse stories about her employer. Extra-marital affairs, unscrupulous treatment of business rivals, tales of corrupt deals and unfairly dismissed employees. All stories which suggested to Yvette that, just because she'd managed to stay on the right side of him, John Harrington hadn't necessarily been 'a good man'.

Someone had killed him for a reason, after all.

She forced herself to concentrate on what she was saying, the words tasting suddenly bitter in her mouth. 'If anyone has any questions,' she continued, trying her best to look as approachable as possible, 'then please speak to your team leader, or by all means come to see me.'

She thought about her own existence, her comfortable life with Quentin. Her husband worked as a solicitor, making them both high earners in a low-income area like this. Their jobs afforded them a nice big house, filled with lovely furniture. Regular overseas holidays in the sun. A cellar with plenty of red wine in it. Two beautiful children.

Quentin was someone's boss, too. What if somebody walked into her husband's workplace one day with a knife, some disgruntled former client or employee, or an escaped psychopath? What if there were rumours about Quentin too, secrets she didn't know; perhaps some shady business dealings she was blissfully unaware of, or the irate spouses of women he was sleeping with behind her back?

Yvette didn't know John Harrington's wife, but she felt suddenly very sorry for her. She also felt an overwhelming desire to retreat to the sanctuary of her office, and decided to end her speech.

'Otherwise, it's back to work as normal,' she concluded. 'Your team leaders will lead you out to your work areas now. Thank you, everyone.'

She waited to see if there was any response, but the group dissipated quietly, as if shell-shocked by the announcement. Feeling surprisingly shaken herself, she turned and headed to the lift, still thinking about John Harrington, and about how quickly a perfect life could unravel.

The rest of the morning was mercifully uneventful. She'd expected a visit from Giacomo, but thankfully the Italian failed to materialise, and Yvette wondered if the obnoxious lackey had left immediately after the briefing. Yet even without further distractions, she'd still struggled to concentrate. She made a couple of calls, left a couple of voicemails. She looked at some samples of paving for the bit of public realm they needed to refresh as part of the deal H and B had struck with the council when the developer acquired the derelict site. She reorganised her desk. After several hours, Yvette had to concede that she wasn't achieving very much at all.

She couldn't get the image of John Harrington out of her mind. She kept imagining his tall frame perforated by stab wounds, bleeding to death on the floor of his office while he called in vain for help, a knife driven again and again into his guts. For some reason she also couldn't shake the idea that Ian Braithwaite was involved. She'd only met the little man a handful of times, but there was something about him that had always unsettled her. Harrington was loud, unpredictable, charismatic; Braithwaite preferred to hover in the background, as though his skin was partially chameleonic, blending into the scenery to better enable him to study you with those penetrating, orb-like eyes.

Get a grip, Yvette; this isn't a murder mystery story, and even if it was, you aren't bloody Poirot.

A knock at her door yanked her back to the present.

'Come in,' she intoned, determined to portray the calm and collected exterior becoming of a senior development executive. *Getting into character*, as her husband sometimes called it.

The petite frame of Leannah Ryan slid into her office, smiling apologetically. Leannah was a recent hire who'd impressed Yvette so far, including when she'd stood up to the patronising, pale, stale and male crew of senior construction managers in a recent design meeting. 'Hi,' said the young woman, her Irish accent pleasant and distinctive.

'How can I help you?' Yvette asked, returning her smile.

'I'm sorry to bother you,' her visitor said, 'but I was wondering if I could chat to you about the designs for the apartment interiors.' Leannah approached Yvette's desk gingerly, brandishing a sheaf of papers. 'I know it's detail, but the specs for the kitchenettes don't seem right to me, and I was hoping to get your approval to look at some different options. I know a few suppliers, and I think we could get better worktops that are also cheaper–'

Yvette's door swung open again, and Giacomo strode into the room, looking like a model stepping straight out of a menswear magazine. 'I need to speak to you,' he said curtly, interrupting Leannah mid-sentence without even looking at her.

'As you can see, I'm busy right now, Giacomo,' Yvette said icily. 'Perhaps if you'd scheduled a meeting...?'

The Italian waved a hand disdainfully. 'I'm sure you realise how busy we are at the moment, especially with what's happened this morning. No, I'm afraid you'll need to continue this discussion some other time.' His eyes flicked across Leannah as though she was a bothersome insect. 'I have some urgent requests from Mr Braithwaite, which need to take priority.'

A battle of wills. Much as Yvette wanted to tell Giacomo that he could bloody well wait his turn, she was aware of how uncertain her position had suddenly become. Harrington had hired her, and promoted her. But now he was dead. That meant Braithwaite wasn't someone she could afford to antagonise.

Which meant his odious assistant held all the cards.

She turned to her subordinate, trying to will a smile onto her face. 'I'm sorry, Leannah. I'll call you as soon as I'm done.'

'Of course,' the design manager replied politely. But Yvette couldn't help sensing her employee's disappointment as she left the office, feeling as though she'd somehow let her down.

6

LEANNAH RYAN

(DESIGN MANAGER, HARRINGTON AND BRAITHWAITE PROPERTY GROUP)

The rest of Leannah's day ebbed by in a strange, surreal haze, and she struggled to concentrate on her work. The news about John Harrington was so shocking that she felt she was in a dream, and she wished she was still lying in bed with Wayne, her brain clinging to sleep and conjuring weird nonsense while she snoozed her alarm clock.

To make matters worse, the exchange with Yvette and the creep from head office had made her feel utterly unimportant. Yvette did eventually email her to ask if they could reconvene early in the morning, and Leannah had said yes, of course they could; but she couldn't help feeling pretty demoralised. She could tell her boss was trying her best to be supportive and encouraging, and to make her feel appreciated, but the disrespect with which she'd been dismissed by the man in the suit – Giacomo, was it? – had revealed her true place in the pecking order.

In the end, she'd left the site shortly after five, hoping to cheer herself up by catching Wayne before he left for work. It was already dark as she drove, taking the longer route so she didn't have to endure a journey through the town centre and witness its dereliction. Axton's high street was always a depressing reminder that, however pleasant her little leafy street on the outskirts was, the town was largely a complete shithole.

Why Axton? Her friends back in Dublin had asked her that on more than a few occasions. Even her parents had started saying things like 'when are you thinking about coming home?', as though her chosen place of residence couldn't possibly be anything other than a short-term stopgap. She sometimes wondered if that applied to their view of her relationship too, although she knew her ageing, religious mum and dad were an easy target when it came to flinging accusations of racism around. They'd never explicitly said that Wayne being black was an issue for them, even as the years ticked by and they realised that her relationship with him was more than just a university romance, that it might soon lead to marriage, even kids.

Either way, she was determined to make it work here in Cheshire. It wasn't that Wayne had refused to relocate; it was that his existence here seemed so full, so rich and teeming with supportive friends and family members. A life suffused with warmth that was so unlike her stiff, stilted, only child's upbringing that she couldn't bring herself to remove him from it. It would be like finding a beautiful butterfly fluttering in the woods and deciding to take it home to pin it to the wall.

She almost smiled at the thought of Wayne being called a butterfly. Then she remembered the morning's macabre developments, and the contempt with which she'd been treated, and her face fell. The car cruised on, rain spattering her windscreen as if the weather was reciprocating her mood.

When she arrived home, she found Wayne already at the door, fumbling his arms into the sleeves of his coat, looking smart in his uniform. He worked as a waiter at the Silver Birch, one of the town's few decent restaurants. It was part of his new plan to reinvent himself as a chef. Wayne had worked in a bar for years, content but unstimulated, happy but poor, so Leannah was delighted he was finally trying to make something of himself. She was even more delighted at his recent culinary pursuits, because his always-impressive cooking was getting really bloody tasty.

'You won't believe this,' he said excitedly as she stepped inside. 'Guess who's made a reservation for tonight, in the private room?'

She'd already told him about her own shocking day during her lunch break, so she'd rather he'd kissed her, held her, asked her about it, before launching into his own story. But she knew she was being needy, troubled by the events at her workplace. 'Who?' she asked, trying to muster some enthusiasm.

'Eric Potter!'

'Err... who's that?'

'You know, the local MP! I might end up serving him if I get a move on; his reservation's at seven.'

'Ah, right, okay,' she replied. 'You know politics isn't really my thing.' Her boyfriend had become more politically active in recent years, so the prospect of meeting Potter in person probably meant a lot more to him than it would to her.

'I know he isn't exactly Barack Obama, but still,' her boyfriend continued. 'I've never served a celebrity before!'

'Sounds like we're both having weird days,' she said.

That seemed to finally remind him about her own tumultuous workday. He hugged her, stooping to kiss her forehead. 'Sorry. Yeah, wow, crazy stuff at your place,' he said. 'Did they tell you anything more about what happened to him?'

She shook her head, feeling suddenly exhausted by the whole horrible business. 'There are rumours going around that he was murdered,' she said, shaking her head in disbelief. 'Apparently he was at Brookhaven Hall, working late, and someone broke in with a knife. But that could all be gossip. I don't know.'

She wished he didn't have to leave, and they could sit on the couch together, watch some Netflix and push all the craziness out of her mind. But Wayne was already saying his goodbyes and hurrying out. 'Your tea's in the oven, and it should still be warm!' he called, as he disappeared around the street corner.

'Love you!' she shouted back, but he was gone. She closed the door, wondering what Wayne had whipped up. She hoped whatever it was would take her mind off thoughts of mutilated bodies and knife-wielding killers.

7

WAYNE MORGAN

(WAITER, THE SILVER BIRCH RESTAURANT)

Guilt chewed at the inside of Wayne's stomach, as it had done for months now, like a particularly voracious parasite that swam and frolicked in his gastric juices. He tried to ignore it as he walked briskly, breath misting in the chill evening air, but it was impossible.

He wanted to split up with Leannah. He couldn't talk to anyone about it; his family loved her, his work colleagues all thought they were a 'great couple', and his friends viewed them so much as a single unit that they called them 'Wayannah', and expressed surprise when either turned up to an event without the other in tow.

If he broached the subject, he knew what people would say: they would ask why he wanted to split with her, and he wouldn't be able to answer. They'd ask if there was someone else involved, and he'd say no. They'd ask what she'd done to upset him, and he'd say nothing, because she was as supportive and thoughtful, funny and beautiful as always. If any of them were insightful enough to ask if he was happy, even then he wouldn't be able to provide a satisfying explanation, because he *was* happy – but in a way that felt, somehow, like a compromise.

A life working towards nothing more than middle-income jobs, children, evenings in front of the TV. A life that was fine but... *flat.*

Mundanity, as an aspiration.

Perhaps he was swept up in his new career, the idea of a job in a restaurant in London or New York or Kyoto, a life of endless potential. Perhaps he was a dreamer, like his parents had always told him, especially when they'd attended parents' evenings to listen to a procession of teachers describe him as a bright and well-mannered boy, but one that struggled to pay attention in class. But still, he couldn't shake off the sense of being at a forked junction, and more and more strongly he felt the urge to veer off down the dustier, less clear path.

He knew the right thing to do was to tell her it was over, however garbled and illogical his blurted-out feelings might sound. At least it would allow her to move on with her own life before they both got any older. He'd thought about doing it that evening, like he had every day for weeks.

Instead, he'd cooked her some seafood linguine and run off to work.

It didn't help that he had absolutely zero experience of breaking up with someone. Before the two of them had met at university, he'd had precisely one girlfriend, and she'd been the one to end the relationship when Wayne had slept with someone behind her back. He'd felt so terrible after the whole experience, had hated the first squirming dance of the nibbling, gnawing guiltworm so much, that he'd resolved never to do anything like that ever again. Yet somehow his current situation felt even worse. It seemed a betrayal at a spiritual level; an act of cowardice far more reprehensible than some meaningless shag. The guiltworm knew this, and it wriggled gleefully.

He arrived at the Silver Birch, determined to focus on work for the evening. Sure enough, he was assigned to the private room, into which Eric Potter and his companion had been ushered minutes earlier, and forced himself to smile confidently as he brought their menus and asked whether they wanted any water for the table.

As with his cooking, politics was another subject Wayne had become much more interested in over the last decade. He knew he wouldn't get much of a chance to discuss the topic with Potter while he was asking the MP which wine he'd prefer with his beef brisket, but still, it was interesting just to see the politician – for whom Wayne was about to vote in a third consecutive election – in the flesh for the first time.

Potter was a controversial figure, loud and opinionated, an outspoken MP who had committed more than a few public blunders over the years. Sometimes he seemed to wilfully seek out quagmires into which he could splat his oversized foot: subjects as widely varied as trans rights, prison reform and mad cow disease had landed him in hot water with his party, and helped to secure his place as a perennial back-bencher. He was right at home there, heckling and shouting like a foreman in one of the mines whose closure he'd once so violently opposed. Never entrusted with a big job in Blair or Brown's government or the subsequent Shadow Cabinet, he'd always been relied upon to hold his seat in the 'red wall' in the constituency where he'd grown up.

Until now. The Axton and Middlewich seat was one of the favourites to fall to the bright young Tory candidate, Nigel Hawke, as an unexpected wave of Brexit-fuelled, pro-Conservative sentiment swept through Labour's former bastions.

Potter certainly looked like a man feeling the squeeze. His face was almost the same livid red as the tie that hung slackly around his neck, loosened as though to relieve some mounting pressure. It wasn't warm inside the restaurant, but Potter's skin looked clammy with sweat, and he dabbed at his brow with his napkin as he perused the food options. The menu looked like a Post-it note in his large, flabby hands.

'I'll have the, err, the pâté to start, and then the pork belly,' he said, appearing flustered. 'And a pint of Guinness, please.'

'Certainly,' Wayne replied. 'And what about you, sir?'

Sitting across from Potter was an odd-looking man that Wayne didn't recognise. He was much smaller than his companion, and the frame hidden inside his charcoal-coloured suit was so slight that it made the shirt and trousers look like empty garments were dangling from the tightly-knotted black tie at his neck. His head, conversely, was oddly bulbous, eyes bulging outwards from it as though it was a balloon over-filled with helium. The overall effect was akin to one of the badly-stuffed Guy Fawkes dummies Wayne had seen lying around the town over the past few weeks.

'Mushrooms on toast,' the man hissed in a voice like escaping gas. 'And the grilled swordfish.'

'And to drink?'

'A glass of Riesling, please.'

Leannah's favourite, Wayne thought. The guiltworm unfurled maliciously.

8

ERIC POTTER MP

(LABOUR PARTY POLITICIAN, MEMBER OF PARLIAMENT FOR AXTON AND MIDDLEWICH)

'I killed John Harrington,' said Eric as soon as the waiter had fucked off.

Ian Braithwaite, the dead man's business partner, paused with his wine glass halfway to his mouth. His rat-grey moustache twitched like a frightened animal, looking like it was about to leap off and scuttle for safety. His bulging eyeballs looked even more protuberant than usual, resembling overripe fruit about to burst.

Eric was reasonably happy with the impact of his opening statement.

'He was blackmailing me,' the MP continued, 'which I'm sure you already knew about, you unpleasant little twat. And now he's dead. So if you don't want to end up in the same boat – which I suspect is halfway across the Styx by now – then I suggest you listen very closely to my proposal.'

It was all bollocks, of course. Eric didn't have a clue who'd killed John Harrington. But he reasoned that this was a sensible bluff: either Braithwaite would fall for it, and acquiesce to Eric's demands, or the despicable bastard would have to reveal that he'd been involved in his business partner's murder himself.

Either way it might give Eric some much-needed leverage, a chance to clamber out of the shitswamp he found himself in. His favourite writer, Joseph Conrad, had once said it perfectly.

Necessity, they say, is mother of invention, but fear, too, is not barren of ingenious suggestions.

'I don't know anything about blackmail,' said Braithwaite carefully.

'Don't bullshit me, Ian,' Potter snapped. 'I want those photos: the originals, as well as any copies you've got. I'm giving you until tomorrow night. We'll meet again, you'll hand them over, and that way you won't end up with a knife stuck in your scrawny guts.'

The knife was a clever little detail. Braithwaite probably knew about the stabbing, being Harrington's business associate and part of his inner circle, but the police hadn't released any specifics to the public yet. If Eric knew such undisclosed particulars of the slaying, it would imply he must be telling the truth. In reality, the politician had tendrils that snaked all over Axton, and had rustled up the information from a contact in the Cheshire Constabulary. He downed his pint as triumphantly as he could, wiping the froth from his top lip with the back of his sleeve.

Checkmate. Or at least a bloody good opening gambit.

Across from him, Braithwaite finished raising his own glass, his unblinking bug eyes fixed on Eric's as he sipped from it, resembling some ancient vulture sucking moisture from a dried-up riverbed. 'Where would we meet?' he asked, in a voice that put Eric in mind of a reanimated mummy. 'Here?'

Eric hated to admit it, but he'd actually preferred dealing with Harrington. 'Somewhere more clandestine. Why not the old coalfield? After all, that's how all this started, isn't it?'

Harrington and Braithwaite had been sore ever since Eric had pulled the plug on the tender for the mine site. Initially the two old swindlers had tried to butter him up, get him to reconsider his intervention, but he'd been steadfast – it was bad enough that Thatcher had closed the mine back in 1985, and now Eric was expected to roll over and let some greedy developers turn a cherished part of the town's heritage into a stack of posh flats? How would that look to the diehard voters?

Stupidly, he'd allowed himself to be sweet-talked, even accepting Harrington's offer of a night in the Cabin. That was where they'd had the pictures taken. At first he hadn't believed the images existed – not until Harrington emailed them to him, as casually as if he was sharing a funny meme he'd found on Facebook. Eric had felt a cold hand squeeze his heart as he'd stared at the photos. He'd seen himself naked before, but never like that. The two young lasses looked like they were trying to ride some sort of bloated, hairless polar bear.

His voting public – not to mention his wife Dawn, and the kids – would not have seen the funny side.

'Shall we say 8pm for the meeting?' he continued bitterly. 'Face to face, you and me, no representatives?'

Braithwaite's face was as impassive as a stone slab. *What if he genuinely didn't know about the photos*, thought Eric with a start, *and I've just clued him in?* The momentary horror made him accidentally inhale half a new potato, and he started to cough as the waiter re-entered the room.

He continued to hack and splutter as the attendant fussed ineffectually around him, eventually propelling the delinquent chunk of carbohydrate halfway across the room to land in the ornate fireplace. Throughout the ordeal, he was aware of Braithwaite's eyes on him, and of the faint quiver of amusement visible beneath the rat-like facial hair.

'Everything okay with your meeting, was it?' asked Dawn as Eric clambered into bed.

'Aye, love,' he grunted. The incident with the potato had resulted in him getting fifty per cent off the entire bill, which he'd decided to reinvest in a dessert and some more drinks. Braithwaite, perhaps unsurprisingly, had not been keen to stick around, so Eric had ended up dining alone. He now felt full, drunk, and cautiously optimistic about the outcome of his little ploy. The loathsome businessman had certainly seemed rattled.

But, as he drifted into a sleep that would inevitably be interrupted by multiple trips to the toilet – and probably by the terrible, barely-comprehensible nightmares that had been plaguing him in recent months – the doubts returned to torment him.

These were not merely doubts about his present situation. These were the deeper-rooted, existential doubts of a politician who'd fallen out of love with politics. For years he'd been buffeted by the winds of change that swept through his party and through Britain, from the hollow optimism of New Labour to the recent resurrection of radical socialism. Once you'd hammered yourself into a new shape enough times, you stopped caring about fitting into any holes at all. Ironically, that was probably part of the reason for his longevity: even as the party was repeatedly demolished and rebuilt around him, Eric Potter was a constant, considered as dependable as an old, gnarled oak.

In truth, he felt old and gnarled, but far from dependable. More like a specimen infected with deeply-ingrained, irreversible rot, a sort of cancerous apathy that had bled out into every aspect of his life. He hadn't spoken to his three sons for weeks, ostensibly because he and they were equally busy. In reality, he found he just didn't have the motivation to pick up the phone. He loved his wife, but not in a way that stopped him from shagging call girls behind her back. He cared about Axton, and felt a deep connection to the place where he'd been born and built a life – but as he saw it drifting into dereliction and disrepair around him, he struggled to muster the energy to combat its decline. *Trust one of your own to fight for you* was his campaign slogan this time round. In reality, he wondered if even a parachuted-in, public school toff like Nigel Hawke might have more appetite for the battle.

Not only did he feel like a fraud, but now he had the photos to worry about, too. Maybe it would be better if it all came out. He could hand the election to Hawke on a platter to match his silver spoon, retire in disgrace, and fade away. And then what would he have to look forward to? His own cholesterol-induced death? To make matters worse, he couldn't shake the thought that if he'd kept his gob shut, maybe the blackmail threat would have disappeared, dying along with the memory and the black heart of John Harrington. *I suppose I'll find out tomorrow.* He wondered if the return of the photographs would put an end to the bad dreams.

Or maybe his nightmares were just getting started.

Eric awoke the next morning feeling like garbage. His dreams had been particularly troubling, visions of knife-wielding maniacs that woke him at 4am with his heart racing, sweating like an exhausted racehorse. He hadn't been able to get back to sleep after that. *Probably time to cut down on the caffeine*, he thought, as he made himself his first coffee of the day. His wife, Dawn, was usually up before him, but it was his Friday morning surgery that day, and he liked to complete the long drive to the church before the traffic started backing up. It didn't do to keep the rabble waiting too long.

St Wilfrid's had stood since the fourteenth century, and

resembled a miniature castle more than a place of worship. The ancient structure was topped with imposing crenellations, and slitted windows from which he half expected arrows to start raining down upon him as he trudged across the car park. That said, he didn't expect anything specifically adversarial from the assembled busybodies. Other than the photographs, he wasn't aware that he was staring down the barrel of any fresh scandals or humiliations. But it always paid to be paranoid. That's why he had Owen Caulfield meet him in the cemetery before they went inside the church, to brief him on any matters he needed to be aware of, or potential banana skins he might have forgotten about.

'We're expecting the usual crowd,' said his advisor, looking at the list of appointments as they strolled amongst the weather-battered headstones. 'Penelope Stroud will probably be moaning about the pothole in her road again.' Eric rolled his eyes. 'And there's that bloke from the Leisure and Culture Trust, probably asking about the plans for the mine.'

'The hunchback?'

Owen glanced nervously around in case anyone had heard the remark, then nodded. Eric grinned; he liked to keep his neurotic, irritable assistant on his toes. There weren't many other pleasures left to him in life.

'Oh, and some young student called Ayesha Kumari,' Owen continued, scanning down the list.

'Bloody hell; so that'll be more questions about trans people or whatever.'

'Yes, well, just make sure you don't put your foot in it again. If you don't want the teenagers to call you a dinosaur, stop acting like a triceratops.'

Eric raised an eyebrow. 'Are you calling me fat?'

Owen ignored him. 'At least there isn't too much fallout from the cancelled trip to Brookhaven,' he said, changing the subject. 'Obviously the journalists I'd lined up were a bit put out, but they can hardly complain – it's now a crime scene, after all.'

'Have they figured out who killed him yet?' Eric asked as nonchalantly as he could manage. He was conscious that a rapid arrest would significantly undermine the lie he'd sold to Braithwaite.

'Nothing announced,' his advisor replied, looking worried. It took Eric a moment to realise why.

'Oh, I'm sorry – your dad's at Brookhaven, isn't he?' Owen nodded. 'I'm sure it's nothing to fret about,' Eric said reassuringly. 'Your old man will be fine. It won't be some random killer on the loose; I bet a sleazebag like Harrington had a lot of enemies.'

Sleazebag. He thought again of the photographs, imagining that exact word plastered across the front pages of the local papers, maybe even the nationals, next to a picture of his beaming face and a couple of choice snaps. A chill passed through him, as if a spirit had reached up from its nearby resting place to prod him accusingly in the ribs. 'All right, let's get this over with,' he grunted, turning to face the church once again. Like the gravestones that surrounded it, the building was noticeably crumbling: a slow but inexorable dissolution.

Just like my career, thought Eric. *And everything else in this fucking town.*

9

AYESHA KUMARI

(A-LEVEL STUDENT, AXTON COLLEGE)

O MG, *there he is*, thought Ayesha as the MP walked into the hall with a big false smile glued onto his fat red face. She was so nervous she was shaking. She felt like abandoning the whole thing and walking straight out of there, tbh. But, like Tammy had said: this was her initiation. It wasn't *supposed* to be easy. So she had to man up, and stop being so extra.

Her hand closed around the egg hidden in her handbag. She wondered about the timing, about when to go for it. Maybe right away, before he sat down behind his stupid little desk, in front of the stupid picture of his own face, grinning that same stupid sycophantic grin.

No, be patient. Stick to the plan, and wait for your turn.

She was third in a short queue of people, all sitting on bright orange plastic chairs like the ones they used to have at school. She'd thought that arriving at the painfully early time start time of 8.30am would have got her a spot at the front, but the other attendees – all old people and weirdos – must literally have been queueing outside in the cold for the doors to open. Probably appropriate that the surgery was happening in the musty main hall of an old church that looked more like a creepy lunatic asylum.

She jacked the volume on her AirPods, wanting to drown out the sound of the old lady who was blabbering about potholes or something. *Seriously, WTF are you even doing here, Ayesha?* There was hardly anyone else there: only Potter, his assistant or security guard or whatever he was, and the handful of cranks lined up alongside her. What was the use of making a big statement if there was no one there to see it? She should have made Collin come with her to film it – at least it might go viral.

And then maybe you'd get arrested, and your dad would go completely nuts.

Her mind whirled, imagining all manner of disaster scenarios. What if the security guy tackled her to the ground before she'd even unveiled the banner? But she'd practised at home and knew she could set it up in less than a minute – plus she had her cover story ready. *I'm promoting a local charity dedicated to helping young women near the poverty line, and was hoping you'd be kind enough to be photographed to show your support?* Then all she had to do was snap him with the camera before he realised what was really happening, and pelt him with the egg for good measure.

But what if I miss? she thought, hearing her breathing getting louder, trying to force herself to calm down. *Or... what if I don't?* She realised she hadn't really thought through her escape plan after the finale. But there was no one manning the door, nothing stopping her from just running away. The absolute worst-case outcome was that they pressed assault charges; but like Tammy said, they were hardly going to send a teenage activist to jail, especially not a British-Indian one. If there was one thing you could count on from old white politicians, it was that they were terrified of looking like racists.

Ayesha glanced at Potter, who nodded patiently while the

old woman carried on ranting. She was surprised to feel a sudden and unexpected wave of guilt. What did she really even know about him? Politics wasn't her bag, tbh. If she was even more 'h' about it, she didn't even remember the name of the Green Party candidate she was supposed to vote for. But the planet was important, and if Potter had said what he was supposed to have said, he deserved what he was about to get. Maybe she should google it though, to make sure it was definitely true... nahh, Tammy wouldn't get something like that wrong. Tammy was smart, and she was really into the cause. Plus her dad was a big dog in property, so she had insider knowledge about buildings and engineering and all that sort of stuff.

Besides, if Ayesha could get through this, pass her initiation, she'd be able to get more involved in the other stuff the AEM were going to do. Only a year younger than Greta Thunberg, and she'd already be a trusted lieutenant in a proper movement that might change the world. Not only would that be sick AF, but it was certain to get her more TikTok followers.

The old lady had finally stormed off, the smile still plastered across Potter's face as though the two of them had had two completely different conversations. The next person rose from his seat, an oldish white man with a scruffy beard who looked like Richard Branson. God, she was nervous. Maybe she could scrap the banner and go straight to the egging. But then there'd be no picture, no proof she'd even done it at all. Did that even matter? It was all starting to feel like too much of a big deal. Her breathing was getting faster and faster, and she started to worry about her asthma. She stupidly hadn't even brought her inhaler, because she'd needed to leave room in her tiny handbag for the ovoid projectile.

The bearded man suddenly got up and walked out, much

quicker than the old woman had. *Oh shit oh shit oh shit. It was her turn. No backing out now.*

'Miss Ayesha Kumari?' said the assistant, glancing at his clipboard. She stood up, feeling hot and cold at the same time.

'I'm... err... I'm with a group... I was hoping I could...' She couldn't get the words out. They felt like lumps of accidentally-swallowed chewing gum, trying to force their way back up her throat. Panicking, she started to unpack the pop-up banner while the two men exchanged confused glances. *Maybe I can just put it here and take a picture with him in the background.* She tried to concentrate on not hyperventilating, and on clicking the stands into place, managing to unfurl the picture on the floor beneath her. Collin himself had made the image on Photoshop, depicting the Earth with a big crack in it, and Eric Potter's laughing face looming in the background like some supervillain from a Marvel movie.

AXTON ECO MILITIA
ERIC POTTER SUPPORTS FRACKING...
AEM SUPPORTS SAVING OUR PLANET!

Somehow, she managed not to secure it properly. The extendable stand snapped closed on her finger, and she yelped in pain. Nearby, another old lady had hauled herself to her feet, and was heading slowly over to her.

'Here, love, let me help you with that.'

Oh God, this is absolutely cringe. Ayesha shook her head, pulling away from the woman and reaching into her handbag, deciding it would all still be okay if she could just...

Her stomach lurched in horror as she realised her handbag was full of bits of shell and slime. She extracted her hand, staring in disbelief as translucent goo dripped onto the tiled floor. The egg must have cracked, somehow.

FFS – my phone was in there too!

'Is everything all right?' Potter asked. She turned towards him, hand still coated with splattered chicken ovum, feeling like she might be about to burst into tears.

'No it isn't, you... you stupid fracker!' she shouted, and turned to run out of the church. Instead, she tripped on the unsuccessfully-revealed poster, sprawling forwards and upending the glutinous contents of her handbag all over herself.

10

COLLIN TAYLOR

(A-LEVEL STUDENT, AXTON COLLEGE; TRAINEE BARISTA, DEJA BREW)

C ollin was adding the finishing touch to another oat milk cappuccino when Ayesha barged into the coffee shop, looking as if she'd been attacked by Slimer from *Ghostbusters*.

'Err... how did it go?' he asked as she stormed straight over to his espresso machine. Although he was preparing the drinks rather than taking the orders, he still wasn't supposed to chat while he worked; but sod it, it was only Samantha in charge that day, and she didn't give a rat's arse about the place either. The only thing lower than Deja Brew's staff morale was the place's food hygiene rating.

'It was lit,' Ayesha replied saltily. She gave him a summary of what had happened, and he fought hard not to grin as she talked him through her misadventures. The tale culminated in the old lady helping Ayesha fumble her sticky possessions back into her even stickier handbag before she was able to finally run off, so hot with embarrassment that she thought the egg might start to fry.

'If you don't wash that off soon, you're going to stink,' he said, trying to suppress a laugh.

'Yes, I'm aware of that. Can I use your bathroom, please?'

'It's closed,' he said, then realised she might be about to cry. 'I'm only joking! There's a code to get in – here.' He scribbled the digits on the back of a bit of till roll and watched as she dashed into the toilets. The girl was cute, but man, she was scatty; he'd had a feeling her 'initiation' wouldn't go entirely according to plan. He'd asked Tammy if the rite of passage was really necessary when they'd spoken the previous evening.

'It's not about the egging, or even the fracking – it's about testing her commitment,' the AEM's leader had replied sternly. 'I don't want someone joining the organisation just for shits and giggles.'

'But if she goes through with it... you're okay for me to invite her tomorrow?'

'If you seriously think she'll add something to the group, yes.'

'Trust me, she definitely will,' Collin had replied, not adding that Ayesha's main contributions from his perspective were a nice arse and an unintentional gift for comedy.

It was a while before she emerged from the bathroom. He was worried she was going to stomp straight out and never speak to him again, but instead she wandered back across to stand next to his machine. 'So... are you going to college today?' he asked.

'Yeah, I've got media studies this afternoon, so I need to go home first and wash this crap off properly.' She pointed to her hair, which was now tied back in a ponytail that still looked slick with egg juice. 'Do you think Tammy will, you know, fire me, or whatever?'

'Nahh, don't worry, I'll smooth it over with her.' He might as well score some free brownie points. 'We're doing a thing tonight, actually – serious shit, not just throwing eggs. Want to come along?'

Ayesha's face lit up like a phone screen. 'Er, yeah, sure... where?'

Samantha shouted an order at him, and Collin rolled his eyes theatrically for Ayesha's benefit before he started work on the skinny flat white with an extra shot. 'A few of us are meeting at the H and B construction site after it's closed, at about nine, nine thirty. I could... pick you up, maybe?' His pulse rate spiked, and he concentrated on adding the little frothy swirl to the coffee.

'Okay, yeah, whatever,' she replied. He glanced up at her, their eyes meeting awkwardly for a moment before she pretended to be looking at her phone, which he could see was switched off and still smeared with goo. 'What is it we're doing anyway?'

'Can't tell you yet. But let's just say the AEM will definitely be getting some attention. We might even make it into the papers tomorrow.'

Ayesha looked up at him again. 'For reals?'

In all of his eighteen years, Collin had never felt quite so cool before. 'For reals. Look, I suppose I'd better get back to work. But... I'll call you later, yeah?'

Ayesha shrugged, but seemed to be hiding a smile as she walked out. *You might actually pull this off,* Collin thought to himself as he watched her go. He hoped so – he liked her, and it would be good to take his mind off Tammy Braithwaite. It might even make her jealous. He knew his mates all thought he was only getting into the whole 'green' thing because of his obsession with Ian Braithwaite's daughter. He'd already gotten loads of grief for dropping out of their Friday night PUBG session again; Max had even called him a simp! *Fucking nerds.* At least he was outside, hanging out with girls at the weekend, while they were all still insulting each other's mums through Xbox headsets.

'SKINNY FLAT WHITE FOR DAVE!' he bellowed, feeling suddenly annoyed. A hipster with a hipster moustache trundled over to collect the drink. Behind him, a blonde woman was also approaching the counter; she was carrying the coffee he'd already served her, which meant she was probably about to complain that he hadn't put enough chocolate sprinkles on it or something.

'Can I talk to you?' she asked in an authoritative tone.

'Err... yeah, sure,' he answered, looking at her properly. She was oldish but not bad looking, wearing a white shirt and brown blazer. Sort of like a hot teacher.

'My name's Ursula, and I'm a police detective,' she said. *Oh no*, thought Collin, his lustful thoughts instantly evaporating. 'I'm investigating the murder of John Harrington. You've heard about that, I assume?'

He nodded. His colleagues had been talking about it as they opened up the shop that morning. Some local businessman, found dead in his office.

'I couldn't help overhearing your conversation,' the woman continued, 'about meeting to do some "serious shit" at his construction site tonight. Would you mind telling me a little more about what that might involve?'

Collin's mouth felt suddenly dry. Samantha barked another coffee order at him, and he filled the portafilter with fresh grounds, working mechanically while he talked.

11

TAMMY BRAITHWAITE

(A-LEVEL STUDENT, AXTON COLLEGE)

'And you just fucking *told her?*'

Tammy had emerged from the shower seconds before Collin rang, and a pair of towels were still wrapped around her midsection and her short, bleached hair as she stalked from the bathroom back to her bedroom with the phone clamped to her ear. She noticed the door to her parents' bedroom was open, the room empty. Her dad was doubtless already at work and her mum was probably lounging in the basement pool, drinking in spite of the early hour.

'What was I supposed to do? She's a bloody police detective! And I told her *where*, but not exactly *what.*'

Tammy felt her hand closing into a fist, nails digging into her palm. 'Why did you say anything at all? You could have said she'd misheard, or it was just a ploy to get your new GF in the car with you, anything!'

'Ayesha isn't my girlfriend.'

'*I don't care*, Collin! The planet is more important than your love life, and it's more important than having to tell a few lies to a policewoman. Climate change is going to wipe us all out; if we want to stop it, we need to make sacrifices! This is a *war!*'

Her friend fell silent, and she removed the phone from her ear, glancing at the screen to check he hadn't hung up. He was still there; her telling off had evidently rendered him speechless. *Good.* She put the phone down on her dressing table and switched the call to speaker while she aggressively dried her hair. *Why couldn't she rely on anybody?* She stared into the mirror, at the googly eyes that she hated, eyes that reminded her of her dad. He'd seemed pretty upset when he got home last night, the row with mum even more vicious than usual. When Tammy had woken up in the middle of the night and gone to get a glass of water, she'd heard him still awake in his study, talking agitatedly on the phone. John Harrington's death must have hit him hard, even though the two of them hadn't been getting along for years.

Don't feel sorry for him, she reminded herself. *Capitalism is the enemy, and people like your dad are its willing agents.*

She glanced around at her huge, expensively-decorated bedroom, and felt like a fraud. Imagine if any of her YouTube followers could see her now; she'd be cancelled faster than R Kelly.

'I guess... we might need to scrap it?' Collin said tentatively. 'We could meet for drinks instead tonight, maybe?'

'What *exactly* did you tell the police we were planning?' she asked, ensuring her tone was as barbed as possible.

'I just said we were going to vandalise it a bit, maybe leave some graffiti.'

Tammy clenched her jaw. 'Then we can still go ahead. We just need to think of a different place to do it. They won't be able to connect us or prove anything that way.'

'Okay... but where?'

There was a knock at her door. 'I don't know. Let me think about it. Look, I'll call you later, I've got to go.'

She hung up as the door cracked open. 'For God's sake, Mum, do I need to get a lock installed? I'm getting changed in here!'

Her mum didn't bat an eyelid. 'Don't you snap at me, young lady. I was only going to ask if you wanted to come with me to the spa. I thought you might want to spend some time with your mother for once.'

'You know I hate that place,' Tammy replied coldly. 'Anyway, I have college.' This was only a half-lie; she did have lessons scheduled that afternoon, but wasn't planning to attend them.

'Yes, but I thought you might be upset after your Uncle John... died so suddenly. I know your father and I are very shocked. I'm sorry if last night we got a bit upset.'

Got a bit upset. Jesus, it was as if her mum truly believed she could dismiss their constant, blazing rows as occasional marital squabbles, part of a normal healthy relationship. Tammy wasn't an idiot. She knew her parents' marriage was as toxic as car exhaust fumes. 'He wasn't my uncle,' she responded icily. 'Anyway, I'm going to be late, so if that's all...?'

Her mother's face, already stretched by countless facelifts, tightened sourly. She turned without a word, slamming the door behind her so hard that the framed photo hanging on the back tilted to one side. Tammy stared at the picture: a herd of African elephants with one infant being doted on by the older members of the group. She wondered what it felt like to have a normal relationship with your family. People thought her life here was easy, in this big house with no money troubles, with no need to get a part-time job in a coffee shop like Collin. A tear dared to venture out from the corner of her eye, and she wiped it away angrily, returning her gaze to the mirror as she began to apply some dark make-up.

Today felt like a goth day.

Minutes later, when she was happy her make-up matched her mood, she headed downstairs, hearing her mother doing something in the living room. She walked quietly past the door, hoping her mum wouldn't try to talk to her again as she edged by. But her mother was distracted, concentrating on sweeping up some broken fragments that were scattered across the floor, and Tammy was able to slip past without another caustic exchange.

Good. She had more important stuff to worry about. She felt her lip curl disdainfully as she closed the front door behind her. All these people, with their trivial concerns, their meaningless worries and disputes, oblivious to the big picture and the poetic justice that was closing in on them. What did any of their problems matter if the planet turned against them? Who would care about career progression or share prices or the latest celebrity scandal when the temperatures became intolerable, when humankind was drowned by the same oceans they'd been thoughtlessly pumping plastic and industrial waste into for decades?

Tammy felt rage simmering within her as she walked. *Good.* She took out her headphones and attached them to her phone, then searched Spotify for Public Image Ltd, who she'd discovered recently, and who reminded her that anger was an energy.

12

FIONA BRAITHWAITE

(RETIRED FLIGHT ATTENDANT)

F iona watched her daughter through the window as she left, gritting her teeth as tears filled her eyes once again. She tipped the shards into the bin, downing the remainder of her wine before she headed out to the car.

Fine. If you don't want to come with me, I'll go by myself.

Their house was out in the countryside, a good twenty-minute drive from town, but this was still not far enough for her liking. She hated Axton, hated that Ian's job had tied them to this stagnant cesspool of a place. Thankfully her destination that morning was in the opposite direction, and she pressed her foot to the accelerator as if she was trying to escape from something.

The trees, and the road that twisted amongst them, kept blurring as she drove, a smear of orange and grey beyond the seemingly unstoppable flow of her tears. The colours reminded her of her body, and its failings: orange, thanks to too much time on the sunbed, which she knew she needed to cut down on, and grey like her hair, with roots that were in desperate need of a touch-up. She wiped her eyes, hoping her make-up wasn't smudged, knowing she should slow down; not only because of the poor visibility, but also because she was probably over the limit after a couple of glasses of pinot that morning. She didn't care. She wanted to get to what felt like her only safe haven in the entire stinking region, as quickly as possible.

John was dead. She still couldn't believe it. She'd only seen him, what, four nights ago? He'd been his usual self: demanding, eager, treating her like a chunk of meat. The way that made her feel alive, and young again. The way she enjoyed, or at least the way she felt she deserved. He'd even ripped her blouse, which might have warranted an elaborate cover story when she arrived home if Ian hadn't already been in bed. Not that she really cared what her husband thought anymore. She was pretty sure he already knew what was going on. If he wasn't such a pathetic weasel, she might even have suspected he was involved in the killing.

Killing. God, how awful. She choked back a sob as she imagined John, a knife skewering his abdomen, piercing the hairy belly she had touched, caressed, watched rising and falling as he slept next to her. Had she imagined the hint of relish in her husband's voice as he'd told her what had happened to his business partner?

Ian had apparently found out the details directly from John's widow, Kim. Fiona wondered if Ian and Kim were perhaps screwing each other too, a sort of perverse mirroring of her and John's affair. Maybe they'd even started first. She hoped so, because that would alleviate the guilt she felt. Not guilt towards her wretched husband, the man who had trapped her in this godawful excuse for a town, but towards Tammy, the daughter who hated her guts, who looked at her through that stupid black make-up as if her eyes could pierce straight to her mum's rotten core. Maybe they could. Maybe Tammy knew about the affair, too. Maybe the whole town did, and called her a slut and a trollop behind her back.

Sod them all, she thought. *I need a drink.*

The sign for the Middlewich Hotel and Spa appeared on the left, signifying that she'd left the immediate vicinity of Axton and entered its neighbouring town. She felt herself relax internally. Here was everything she needed to get through the day: a Jacuzzi, a masseuse, and a bar. Even the approach felt better, the neatly manicured trees along the drive like attendants lined up to welcome her, instead of the ugly and bedraggled husks that skulked beside the main road. She ought to talk to Potter about getting the council to trim them back properly.

In fact, wasn't that who Ian had been out drinking with last night? Her husband had come back from the meeting in a foul mood. Everything would be better when that nice Mr Hawke won the election, she remembered saying; that was when she'd still been trying to calm him down, before their exchange had rapidly deteriorated. Not that a switch of MP would do anything to improve this dump of a town, or to fix their marriage.

She scowled as the haze of her memory coughed up more fragments of the previous night's argument. Ian had been unusually vicious, at one point even calling her a 'hateful bitch'. She remembered, suddenly, the momentary rage that had flared in his eyes when she'd retorted by saying he had 'little man syndrome'. She'd honestly thought he might hit her. In some ways she would have been impressed that he'd shown a bit of backbone for once.

No, that wasn't true. He'd scared her last night. He'd been angrier than she'd ever seen him. Part of his rant came back to her, suddenly and vividly. 'All this,' he'd snarled, sweeping his arm as though to indicate the house, their possessions, their entire life. 'It's ephemera. It can unravel so fast you don't know what's hit you.' He'd swept the vase off the mantelpiece, a wedding gift from her dead aunt. The sound of it shattering on their recently laid stone tiles had made her jump.

'Just ask John,' Ian had said, with a gruesome smile she didn't remember seeing before.

She felt herself shudder as she pulled into the car park, stopping the car skewed across two spaces, her hands trembling too much for her to correct it.

13

NICOLAS MUÑOZ

(FRONT DESK CLERK, MIDDLEWICH HOTEL AND SPA)

Nicolas saw her walk in, and sighed to himself. Mrs Braithwaite: the wealthy woman with almost as much plastic surgery as he was used to seeing back in South America, the drinking habits of a sailor, and the manners of a wild boar. He was pleasantly surprised when she didn't try to push her way straight to the front of the queue, which was a tactic she'd tried before.

He was already feeling stressed enough without having to deal with the old harpy. It had been unusually busy in the hotel that day, and thanks to a colleague's alleged illness, he was having to man the front desk alone, taking bookings for the spa as well as checking guests in and out. To make matters worse, there had already been some particularly unsavoury customers. First, there was Mr Ademola, the shifty-looking man who'd looked like he was trying to hide inside his shabby, oversized trench coat. He'd paid extra for an early check-in and had glanced around nervously while Nicolas processed his details.

Now, standing at the front of the queue was what could only be described as a monster. Well over six feet tall and somewhere in his forties, the man's huge arms hung by his sides like a pair of tree trunks, a tracery of tattoos emerging at his wrists from beneath the black long-sleeved sweatshirt he wore. His bald head was all sharp angles and protruding ridges as though he was using a piece of old rock for a skull. When the enormous newcomer took a massive stride towards his desk, Nicolas half expected the entire building to shake.

'Can I help you?' he ventured with a polite smile when the colossus didn't say a word.

'Checking in,' said the man in an odd accent. Nicolas had been in the UK for a while now, after becoming the favourite Argentinian souvenir of a British backpacker six years ago. Yet despite Wesley's attempts to educate him on the difference between Scousers, Brummies and Cockneys, he still found them all indiscernible (and often incomprehensible).

'Okay, sir. What name is that?'

Now that he was standing closer, Nicolas could see that the man's eyes had a distant, haunted look, as though he was gazing straight through him. In fact, he seemed to be staring right through the wall behind him, through the entire hotel, to somewhere deep in the forest beyond. The sensation was a strange one, like being addressed by someone who thought you were a ghost.

'Torrance,' the man replied, his voice hollow and empty, putting Nicolas in mind of a machine impersonating a person. *He's probably on drugs*, he thought. *Great, just what we need on the premises: a strung-out bodybuilder*. He scanned the list of reservations, hoping that the name wasn't there and that the musclebound oddball had made a mistake; but sure enough, there he was. Harry Torrance, with a reservation for one night.

'Ah yes, very good, sir,' Nicolas said, conjuring a smile. 'But I'm afraid your room won't be ready until 2pm.'

Torrance blinked once, slowly, managing somehow in that single movement to convey immense disappointment but also resignation. A solemn acceptance that railing against the world and its capricious whims was utterly, crushingly futile.

Nicolas had never seen anyone who looked so sad.

'Where can I wait?' Torrance intoned.

'Well sir, the main bar is just downst–'

'I don't drink,' Torrance interrupted. He said it in a way that suggested terrible, unspeakable things might happen if even a single drop of alcohol was to pass between his lips.

'Okay... um, well if you'd rather not sit in the bar, I can perhaps recommend the waiting area right over there.' Nicolas smiled resolutely as he gestured towards the pair of sofas in the nearby corridor, opposite the lifts. 'I'm afraid we're in a bit of an out of the way spot, so there isn't much else to do nearby, but if you have a car you could always drive to Middlewich, which is known for its–'

'The waiting area's fine,' the man interrupted. As he paced slowly towards the couches, Nicolas wondered if his reply meant he didn't have a car with him. *If not, how the hell did he get here?* Maybe he was military, or something, and had hiked through the woods. Nicolas could certainly believe it. He watched Torrance lower himself into a seat like a tank being airlifted into place. The gargantuan man didn't produce a phone, or a book to read, or any other way to pass the time. He simply sat there, hands flat on his thighs, staring straight ahead at the opposite wall.

Or through it, to some darkness beyond.

'Excuse me,' said the next customer, startling Nicolas out of his reverie.

'Oh, yes, I'm terribly sorry,' he said, quickly recovering the smile that he realised had faded from his face.

Next in the queue at the reception desk was a gaunt woman whose blouse and cotton trousers were as black as her hair, the dark glasses she wore completing her funereal aesthetic and contrasting starkly with her lily-pale skin. The only way she could have looked more like a Hollywood femme fatale was if she was puffing at a cigarette in a long holder.

'I'm Kimberley Harrington,' she said brusquely. 'Here to meet with Patrick Ademola, who I believe has already checked in.'

Something about her name tugged at a corner of his brain – had he met her before?

'Er, certainly, ma'am,' he replied, searching the computer to check he had remembered the room number correctly. He wondered what such an urbane creature could possibly want with the grubby, furtive Mr Ademola. They were probably about the same age – older than Nicolas, perhaps a similar age to the possibly-military man who was still directing his eerily vacant stare into the space between the lifts – but the idea that this was a rendezvous for midday sex seemed about as plausible as Fiona Braithwaite being there to order non-alcoholic prosecco.

Wait – *Harrington and Braithwaite* – that was it! This slender, porcelain-skinned specimen was the wife of the businessman that had died two nights ago. Nicolas wondered whether her dark attire was a reflection of her state of mourning, or if it was her usual choice of wardrobe. 'Would you like me to ask Mr Ademola to come down to meet you?' he asked.

'It's a private meeting,' she replied curtly. 'I'll head up to his room. What number is it?'

He knew he ought to phone Mr Ademola to confirm whether this was acceptable, but the queue behind Mrs Harrington was getting longer by the minute, and her demeanour suggested he'd come to deeply regret it if he messed her about. 'Of course,' he smiled. 'He's in 312, on the top floor. You can take the lift just over there.'

She turned without a further word, paused for a moment,

then walked towards the elevators. Nicolas watched her, wondering if a pretty woman crossing his field of vision would yield some flicker of emotion from the seated Harry Torrance. It didn't.

Nicolas turned to the next customer, activating his broad smile once again. *Perhaps this line of work isn't so bad*, he thought as he admitted a visitor to the spa. *At least hotels are always full of interesting people, and their interesting secrets.*

He saw Mrs Braithwaite lurking next in line, and his smile quickly dissolved.

14

KIM HARRINGTON

(VOLUNTEER CHARITY WORKER)

T he sight of Fiona Braithwaite in the queue stopped Kim in her tracks for a second. Her stomach somersaulted, the acid tang of loathing flooding her mouth so suddenly that she almost gagged. But she gritted her teeth and ignored the tangerine-skinned bitch, who at least afforded her the same courtesy; a false smile and some vacuous words of condolence from Fiona Braithwaite would have been too much to bear.

She summoned the lift, ignoring the weird Neanderthal in the chair behind her, willing it to descend as quickly as possible so she could escape from the painful awkwardness of the situation. She should have known that Fiona would be a regular patron at a place like this. She was probably shagging her tennis coach, or some musclebound massage therapist.

Maybe that's why I hate her so much, Kim thought, as the elevator disgorged an elderly couple and she stepped inside to take their place. It wasn't the fact that John had been sleeping with someone behind her back. It was that he'd chosen to do it with someone like *Fiona*: a bottle-blonde, plastic bimbo whose breast implants had probably trebled her IQ the moment they were installed. *Still clever enough to land herself a rich husband,*

and then seduce yours too, Kim's brain chided her, making her scowl. She remembered the early meetings between the four of them, the uncomfortable 'double dates' she'd had to endure before John's relationship with Ian had soured like bad milk. Fiona had always drunk too much wine and cackled like a demented witch at everything John said, leaving Kim to try to make small talk with Ian, a man so creepy and unsociable that trying to coerce a conversation out of him felt akin to necromancy.

He'd called her yesterday to express his condolences and to agree how they would manage the 'messaging' to the company's staff. She remembered wondering whether he was in the same position she was: knowing about the affair, unsure whether the participants knew that their secret wasn't a secret. Kim's brain had been so scattered she'd almost asked him directly.

Exiting the lift, she followed the signs towards room 312. The third floor's ageing carpets and peeling wallpaper were testament to the hotel's deteriorating financial position. Like Fiona, the Middlewich evidently suffered from delusions about its own beauty and ongoing significance. The situation was exacerbated by the recent opening of a new Premier Inn that had deftly siphoned off the cheaply-suited business travellers that buzzed around Middlewich's data centre like a cluster of persistent flies. Axton and Middlewich: two towns separated by a few miles and by the river Bollin, a narrow strip of sluggish water that acted like a defective magic mirror, presenting a dystopian and decayed vision of a once-proud northern town on *both* sides.

Eric Potter, the local MP who had dominated an unhealthy portion of her husband's thoughts in recent months, popped into her head. *The king of shit mountain*, John had called him, among an array of other creative unpleasantries. She actually found the old dinosaur quite charismatic, although this was not a fact she'd dared to share with John, who was as militant a Tory voter as you could get.

She couldn't discount the possibility that Potter was involved in her husband's death, of course. Their feud was clearly serious, much more vitriolic even than his endless bickering with Ian. Or was it? Maybe that's why John had been screwing Fiona – not because he had any feelings for the stupid airhead, but because fucking his partner's wife was the ultimate one-up.

Not the ultimate, she realised as she knocked on the door. Perhaps Ian had found out about the affair, and a battle between two alpha males had turned deadly. *Perhaps killing John was Ian's way to win their battle once and for all.*

She saw something flicker at the peephole, and the door cracked open an inch, as though the room's occupant was terrified of being seen. 'Come in,' Patrick hissed, and she heard the rattle of the chain being removed. The door opened just wide enough for her to slip inside, and as she did so she realised how nervous she was. Understandably, perhaps. She'd hired the private investigator to capture images of her husband's infidelity ahead of her plan to divorce him.

Instead, Patrick Ademola had photographed the moment of John Harrington's death.

***

The pictures were laid out on the bed. Kim stared at them with a queasy feeling, her throat clogged while her belly felt like a yawning chasm. For some reason she'd expected the pictures to be in black and white, like they always were in the movies. Instead, they were in colour, with their lurid story laid out like a deconstructed flicker book.

John, seated in an office somewhere, a place she didn't

recognise. His back was to the camera, which had snapped him through the room's only window.

John, now risen to his feet, holding a beige folder in one hand.

John, standing in front of the enormous painting on the right-hand wall.

John, manipulating something behind the picture, which he'd removed and leaned against the wall at his side. She could now see the image it depicted, a full-length portrait of a young man in fine clothes, his lip curled into an arrogant sneer as if he already knew what was about to happen.

John, returning to his desk, the folder now missing, the canvas replaced. He was looking almost straight into the camera, and she felt the clot in her throat expand. A man she had loved, once. A man she had been conspiring against. A man she would never see again. *A dead man.*

John, seated once more.

John, rising again, walking towards the door.

John, leaning forward to peer out through the open entrance.

The room, empty. The impression she got was that John had heard a knock at the door, but found nobody there when he opened it, and so had gone out into the corridor to investigate.

John, reappearing at the door, clutching his stomach. His face had twisted into a grimace, an agonised expression that made her shiver. Even at his mother's funeral – the only time she'd ever seen him cry, the moment when its fleeting absence made her realise that her husband hid his feelings behind a permanent, carefully-polished mask – he had not looked this anguished.

John, pawing at the window as though trying to find a way to escape through it, like an insect baffled by the glass. His futile actions left a bloody smear across the pane. It persisted on the remaining photographs, like a scarlet smudge on the camera lens.

John, slumped in his chair, his expression changed now, closer to the slack-jawed horror she had beheld when identifying him at the morgue. Abyssal eyes gaped above a lolling tongue that looked like something trying to escape from his mouth.

John, still slumped in his chair: an identical photograph, as if to underscore the finality of his last repose.

A final image, this time depicting a uniformed woman appearing at the open door. Her face was contorted into a half-formed scream, hands clapped on either side of the widening 'O', resembling an Edvard Munch painting.

Kim stared, unable to remove her eyes from the picture. 'Why didn't you help him?' she whispered.

Patrick was seated on the other side of the bed, occupying the room's only chair. He'd offered it to her, but she'd declined, preferring to stand; perhaps to give her comfort that she could flee at any moment. The curtains were tightly drawn and the lighting dim, making it seem as if she'd stepped outside of reality when she crossed the threshold, into some dusk-shrouded nightmare realm. 'I'm sorry,' he said. 'I didn't realise what was happening until it was too late. I called the police anonymously, but they told me they were already on their way to the address. The woman who found him must have called them straight away.'

Kim wiped tears from her eyes, replacing her sunglasses like a knight donning their armour. 'Where did this even happen?'

'Brookhaven,' Patrick replied in his usual, matter-of-fact style and faint Midlands twang. 'The care home.'

Like many of John's property developments, Brookhaven was a place she'd never visited. She'd always found it strangely disturbing, that John's job resulted in the appearance of these permanent structures. It seemed somehow obscene that England's landscape was enduringly altered so that they could live in a nice house and drive fancy cars and eat posh food, as if their lifestyle left an indelible mark on the world. Perhaps it would have felt less cynical, less grotesque, if they'd had children. But John was very adamant that he didn't want them.

'And you didn't see who killed him,' she said, a statement rather than a question, because Patrick had already told her as much in their earlier phone conversation.

The PI shook his head. 'I even waited in case I saw someone escaping, but they must have got away from the other side of the building.' She looked at him, this peculiar man she'd found online, advertising his investigative and surveillance expertise. She couldn't explain why she'd chosen him out of all the available firms. Perhaps his website had felt more human, more honest about the seediness of the services he was offering. He hadn't tried to dress up the act of spying on your husband as being as natural and innocuous as hiring a cleaning company.

Maybe what had happened was all her fault. Perhaps by reaching out to interface with Patrick's hidden world, a realm of snooping and subterfuge, she had somehow allowed its dark forces to reach back and violate her own existence. This violence, this evil, was not from her reality; it was from Patrick's, and she'd been stupid enough to think she could control it.

'What was behind the painting?' she asked, trying to maintain her composure.

'A safe,' he replied. 'John put the folder in it a few minutes before... before what happened.'

'Before he was *killed*,' she snapped, angered by the euphemism. Patrick fell silent. 'What was in the folder?'

'I don't know.'

She sensed the investigator had more to say. The air in the room was thick with it. 'Go on,' she prompted.

'I took... other pictures. The sort you wanted.'

'I don't understand.'

Patrick sighed deeply, a sound that seemed to contain within it every photograph he'd ever taken, every sordid encounter he'd witnessed, every crime, every wretched little scam. The sigh of a man who'd spent a lifetime digging in the gutter. 'John had a sexual encounter with a woman, about an hour before these stills were taken. It was the same woman who later found him dead.'

Kim felt the world lurch around her. She reached beneath her glasses to press her fingers into her eyes, feeling an urge to jam the digits deeper, all the way through the orbs and down into the sockets. 'Show me,' she said. She thought Patrick might try to protest, that he'd say she'd had enough, that he'd only shown her the pictures of John's death because she'd insisted, as his paying client. But he didn't say anything; he just nodded wearily, and reached into the satchel at his side. Four more glossy imprints joined the others, each laid carefully on the bedspread as though he were arranging an art exhibition.

Kim felt bile rise in her gullet as she scanned them. This time John was opening the door to that same blonde girl, the one who had found him. She was, what, barely twenty-five?

The next picture showed him returning to his desk, his hands moving towards his belt. Kim's mouth creased in disgust. Patrick's nightmare realm was clearly far from finished with tormenting her.

A third snap depicted John, seated with his trousers around his ankles, the woman fellating him. Kim felt she might vomit.

In the next picture his clothes were back in place, his attention already returned to the paperwork on his desk even though the woman was barely halfway out of the room.

She wondered if these were the only pictures he'd taken, or if Patrick had chosen these as his edited highlights.

'Well,' she found herself saying, after a long quivering breath. *Seems Fiona Braithwaite wasn't the only one.* She realised Patrick was watching her, as though trying to assess her psychological state. 'Just tell me everything,' she said, feeling herself hardening, her flesh replaced by a Kimberley-shaped callus.

Patrick nodded his slow, tired nod. 'I think John was running some sort of prostitution racket. Rich clients, taken out to somewhere in the woods that I haven't been able to find. I followed him that night because I thought that's where he might be going, but instead I ended up at the care home, hidden in the trees with my binoculars and my camera.'

Kim's mouth felt full of ashes. She couldn't stop staring at the photographs, feeling as if she was staring through a window into her husband's soul. It was a more desolate and repulsive place than she'd ever realised. 'I don't... know what I'm supposed to do with this,' she stammered.

'It might be something to do with why he died. And I thought you'd want to know in case any of it comes out. It could damage you.'

There was an unexpected tenderness in Patrick's words. She looked up at him. 'John refused to write a will, you know,' she said, her words seeming to come from someone outside, some other Kim whose world wasn't unravelling like a plucked sweater. 'He said you were supposed to fear death, not plan for it like one of those washed-up old celebrities advertising life insurance.'

'You're his widow. You still have a legal entitlement.'

'But if he was a... a *criminal?*' Her brain was spinning, as if the room was floating in space, untethered from Earth's usual orbit. 'Not just a dodgy businessman, but a *pimp*, or whatever. Couldn't that affect what happens?'

Patrick, so fidgety and uncomfortable when in public,

appeared more at ease in that locked and darkened room. Sitting calmly in the chair in the dim light, cast in shadow, he looked like an effigy chiselled out of obsidian. 'Possibly,' he said. 'It could be a messy process, dividing an estate without a will, in the middle of an ongoing murder investigation.'

Kim returned her gaze to the photographs, this time focusing on the image of John fiddling with the wall behind the portrait. 'I want to know what's in that safe,' she said. 'Can you get into it somehow, before the police find it?'

'I don't know the combination.'

'But you could crack it.'

Patrick shifted uneasily. 'That would be illegal. Plus the police will still be poking around.'

'I'll pay you whatever you want.'

He paused, sucking his teeth. 'I'll have to charge you ten thousand,' he said eventually.

'I'll pay you twenty if you can find out where the place in the woods is, too.' The words felt like she was spitting out icicles.

'Can I ask you something, Mrs Harrington?' he asked, raising an eyebrow. She nodded. 'Why do you care about it?'

She held his stare. 'Because I might want to burn it to the ground.' Silence hung like a pall.

'I'll wait until tonight to try the safe,' Patrick said eventually. 'It's too dangerous during the day.'

'Just call me when you have some news.' She turned and walked towards the door, then stopped. 'And I don't care how bad it is,' she said, before letting herself out.

She heard the lock snicking into place behind her moments later, the rattle of the door chain being reattached as she headed towards the lift. The sounds of paranoia. The lights in the corridor were dazzling after the gloom of room 312, making her glad of her shades.

John, you piece of shit. It sounds like you got what you deserved.

Already her encounter with Patrick felt like a bad dream, a fading nightmare.

But how do I make sure I get what I deserve?

She extracted the card holder from her pocket, locating the details Inspector McKenzie had given her.

Time to find out what the police already know.

15

ABIGAIL MCKENZIE
(DETECTIVE CHIEF INSPECTOR, CHESHIRE
CONSTABULARY)

S miling brightly, DI Friedel lowered himself into the chair on the opposite side of the desk. His hair was almost the same chalky white as his skin, making his blue eyes look like gemstones half-buried in snow. Abigail wasn't sure if he was albino – didn't they all have red irises? – but was waiting for an appropriate time to ask. You could probably get sacked for discrimination for mentioning it these days.

'You wanted to see me, ma'am?' the young detective asked cheerfully.

Abigail was about to reply when her phone rang. She held up an apologetic hand as she removed the device from her pocket, noticing the unknown number and almost ignoring the call. Instead, she answered with her customary greeting. 'DCI McKenzie, Cheshire Constabulary.'

It was Kimberley Harrington, the wife of the businessman who'd been murdered in Axton the previous morning. A woman whom Abigail had accompanied in person to identify her husband's body. 'How can I help you, Mrs Harrington?'

When the mortician had peeled back the sheet, revealing her husband's ghastly death mask, Abigail had been surprised when Kimberley Harrington didn't weep or cry out. She'd simply nodded in silent recognition, and Abigail had realised she'd mistaken the woman's sapling-thin build for weakness.

'I just wondered how the case was going,' the widow said.

Abigail McKenzie was the head police officer assigned to the town of Axton. Given the nature of the crime and the high profile of its victim, the Harrington murder was by far her biggest current case. She intended to solve it, and had been frustrated with the lack of progress in the first twenty-four hours. 'We don't have any concrete updates so far,' she replied carefully, 'but please rest assured that I'll keep you personally informed of developments.'

'So you haven't found anything at the crime scene, or about... about John's business dealings?'

Abigail frowned. 'Was your husband in some sort of difficulty, Ms Harrington?'

'Oh no, nothing like that. I'm just worried, I suppose, that there was something going on that might have implications for his family.'

Abigail's frown deepened. 'Ms Harrington, if there's anything you're aware of, information you aren't sharing with me, you need to let me know. It might be crucial to the investigation. A bad business deal could be exactly what got your husband killed.' Her senses were howling like a sniffer dog's. Decades of policework – of the painstaking cross-checking of information, of combing through crime scenes for blood spatters or discarded clothing, of hours spent fruitlessly interviewing witnesses – had taught her that hunches couldn't always be trusted. Harrington hadn't wept at the sight of the corpse, and now she was calling to ask some slightly odd questions, but that didn't mean she was involved in her husband's murder. Grief manifested in bizarre ways, and detectives cracking cases with flashes of intuitive brilliance only happened in the movies.

Or perhaps not, she thought, eyeing DI Friedel optimistically. He appeared not to be listening, focusing instead on arranging the paperclips he'd removed from the little dispenser on Abigail's desk into a circular pattern.

'I already told the detective everything I know,' the widow replied. 'John's relationship with Ian – his business partner – was pretty unhealthy. That's the only thing I can think of.'

Harrington and Braithwaite, the local property tycoons. Another avenue of enquiry Abigail certainly intended to pursue. 'I'm putting more manpower on the case as of today,' she said, glancing again at her colleague and his impromptu paperclip art piece. *This kid really is a weirdo*, she thought. *But a talented one, by all accounts.* 'So you may need to go through some of that information again in a little more detail, I'm afraid.'

'Oh.' Harrington didn't sound as pleased with this news as Abigail had hoped. 'I mean, the detective I spoke to seemed very competent. There's really no need to go to unnecessary trouble...'

'Please, Mrs Harrington, leave it to us.' Abigail was convinced the dead man's widow knew something she wasn't disclosing. 'I know this is a very difficult time, but the best thing you can do after the terrible shock you've had is to try to rest at home, and help my officers if they need any information from you.'

Harrington was silent for a few moments. 'Look, I'm not saying there's anything specific I'm aware of, but if you do find anything untoward about John... I'd appreciate a heads-up if it's going to become public, that's all.'

'Of course. Contrary to the way we're depicted on TV, we always proceed with the utmost discretion.'

'Okay. Well, thank you for your time.' Harrington hung up before Abigail could say goodbye.

'That was Kimberley Harrington,' she said, stroking her chin.

'I heard,' replied Friedel, without lifting his eyes from his stationery sculpture. 'Almost sounded like she doesn't want us to solve the case. I assume that's what you're planning to assign me to?'

Abigail smiled. 'Bingo. DS Pembridge was the first one at the scene, and she's a good officer, but I need this one in the can as quickly as possible. So you'll be taking over, and she'll be reporting to you.'

'Will she be put out about it?'

'I've already told her, and yes she is, but I also don't care. You're in charge now, so treat her as an extra resource.'

Friedel nodded, leaning back in his chair as though finally happy with the layout of the paperclips. He offered Abigail another of his genial smiles. *A weirdo, but a charismatic one. He'll go far, if he doesn't drop the ball.* 'I'll want to see the scene, too,' he said.

'Fill your boots. Pembridge has been sniffing around Axton since the body was found, so she can give you the guided tour, and bring you up to speed on the specifics.'

'Anything else I need to know?'

'Only that this might get political. I've already had Potter, the MP, on the phone asking for updates. These rich bastards don't half make a lot of waves when they die.'

'That's because they're usually corrupt,' said Friedel, without a hint of irony. 'Should I pay Potter a visit?'

'I doubt he's involved. And besides, the cynical old bastard will probably only try to canvas you for your vote.'

Friedel rose from his seat, tall and gangly, like a person built out of spare elbows. 'I don't do politics,' he replied, and walked smartly out of the office.

Abigail glanced again at the paperclip circle he'd left on her desk, reaching across to sweep them into her cupped hand. She realised as she did so that he'd attached each one to the next, creating a long and unbroken chain that looped back upon itself, the first paperclip connecting to the last.

Reminds me of me, chained to this bloody desk, she thought, and tossed it irritably into the wastepaper bin.

16

TOBIAS FRIEDEL

(DETECTIVE INSPECTOR, CHESHIRE CONSTABULARY)

F riday encircled him, a bright blue wheel with him at the centre, each segment of time discretely visible as if he was wearing a bizarre imaginary tutu. Ahead of him was Saturday, mustard yellow as usual, waiting for midnight to welcome him into its own midpoint; that disc was followed by the burnt umber of Sunday, its segments less clear, before the trail disappeared into a cloud of murky uncertainty that tasted faintly acidic, like the apple bonbons he used to enjoy at the cinema as a child.

Toby was synaesthetic, a condition that affects around four per cent of the population to some extent. It meant that a stimulation of one of his senses or cognitive pathways led to involuntary experiences in other, normally unrelated ones, or – in the simpler terms he used to explain the phenomenon to most people – that for him numbers and words had colours, days of the week existed in physical space, and emotions had distinct tastes. There were many other forms of synaesthesia (apparently at least seventy-three) including everything from flavours experienced as musical sounds to pain having a distinct smell. He still remembered when he'd first found out that his experience wasn't the norm, staggered that other people didn't perceive the world in the same way as him. Their existence sounded so painfully *monochrome* that he felt deeply sympathetic whenever the subject came up in conversation, and his question 'so what does happiness taste like to you?' was met with a baffled stare.

But his coloured 'day wheels' weren't only an interesting talking point – they helped him plan his activities meticulously, each half-hour wedge a narrow window through which he could peer at a visual representation of what he planned to use the time for. In effect, his brain came pre-installed with an instantly accessible, colour-coded diary.

The first thirty minutes of his involvement in the case were used to speak over the phone with DS Pembridge, before driving to the care home where they'd agreed to meet. Her tone on the phone was strained but professional, and he hoped this signalled that an effective working relationship awaited them. In the same way others didn't understand how the days of the year stretched out ahead of Toby like a gaudy production line, he often struggled to fathom the complexities of human interaction, the weird dance of etiquette and near-telepathic politeness that contact with others seemed to require. The protocols of communication were, to him, at best painfully inefficient, at worst utterly bewildering. People often told him they thought he was on the spectrum, as though that was a bad thing.

When he'd told DCI McKenzie *I don't do politics*, he'd meant it in the widest possible sense.

He emerged from the unmarked vehicle as he progressed into the second time unit, the wheel rotating around him (it didn't make a sound as it did this – he didn't have time/sound synaesthesia). This half hour would be spent examining the crime scene. The SOCOs had already finished their inspection, revealing the fingerprints of the deceased and the blood with which Harrington had decorated the room during his death throes. Toby wasn't expecting to find anything the SOCOs' thorough process hadn't already revealed; he just wanted to get a feel for the place where the victim had spent his final moments.

A sullen-looking care worker met him at the doorway. 'The other copper said to take you upstairs,' the man said grumpily. Toby thanked him, flashing the wide grin he'd learned was usually effective at ingratiating him with others. This time, though, the smile wasn't reciprocated. He followed the man upwards, staring at his shock of grubby-looking curly hair, exactly halfway between brown and grey. Toby washed his own hair twice every day, a habit he'd had since his childhood back in Dusseldorf, when the girl he fancied at school had told him he smelt funny. He knew mild OCD could probably be added to synaesthesia and autism on his roster of 'quirks', and couldn't imagine spending every day working in a place as unclean as this, all faeces and vomit and sweat, like a never-ending crime scene.

They turned into a long corridor, and he saw Pembridge waiting for him next to an open doorway about halfway along it. She offered him a stiff good morning as he approached, holding up the police tape so he could duck under it into the room beyond. He'd already quizzed her about her investigation thus far, which sounded like solid police work, so there was little to talk about as he surveyed the scene. He knew she'd interviewed the two women who'd been working the night shift, including the one that had found the body and called 999. He knew she'd completed the formalities of informing the widow, of getting the corpse transferred to the morgue and ensuring it was identified. He knew she'd found no sign of forced entry to the building, and that more junior manpower had been drafted in to assist with the search of the grounds for the murder weapon.

He also knew she'd overheard some local teens chatting in the coffee shop while she'd been reviewing her notes that morning, and that they were planning some sort of environmental protest that same night. Probably a red herring, but he'd already devoted a time segment to following up on it.

But that was later. For now, his attention was focused on scouring his surroundings.

The room was fairly nondescript, all filing cabinets and lever arch files and bland, generic ornaments. Its only noteworthy feature was the enormous portrait hanging on one wall. Aside, of course, from the pool of blood on the floor under the chair, and the smears across the desk and window. Toby wondered if the surly care worker, who he realised was still watching them from the doorway, knew that it was the staff's responsibility to clean up the scene after the police left. It wasn't a detail they usually mentioned in *CSI*.

'What's your name?' he asked the man, whose underbite was so pronounced that he looked like an orc.

'Greg,' the man grunted.

'Well, Greg, a cup of tea would be nice. Milk and two sugars, please. DS Pembridge?'

His colleague looked momentarily taken aback. 'Err, coffee, black, no sugar. Thanks.'

Greg opened his mouth, then closed it, glaring at the two police officers before turning briskly and tramping away down the corridor.

'Can't get the staff,' Toby remarked, and Pembridge smiled. *Well done, Toby. Ice broken, or at least thawed a bit.* 'Has the chair been moved?'

Pembridge shook her head. Toby headed towards it, crouching to look at the blood pooled beneath, the colour of

Tuesdays. He'd seen the photographs of the scene, been unsettled by the dumbfounded shock frozen on Harrington's face. 'Do you think Harrington was stabbed at his desk, or somewhere else?'

Pembridge frowned. 'I suppose I assumed whoever killed him came into his office while he was working, and knifed him right here. Maybe they knew each other, and they sat talking for a bit. That would explain why there was no break-in. Then the killer suddenly pulled out a knife, circled the desk before Harrington could get up and...' She mimed the grisly conclusion of her sentence.

He nodded thoughtfully, scepticism tasting similar to peanuts. 'There's no sign of a struggle in here,' he said, looking at the unbroken vase on top of the nearby filing cabinet, the papers undisturbed on the desk aside from the bloody handprint with which they'd been imprinted like some gruesome signature. He rose and crossed to the door, scanning the insides of the frame.

'They already checked that,' Pembridge said, mild frostiness returning to her tone.

'What about the corridor outside?'

'I don't think so.'

Toby stepped back under the police tape and began to examine the nearby walls, which were white, and the floor, which was covered with the same cardboard-coloured carpet as Harrington's office.

'Don't worry, I already checked whether there was a trail of bloody footprints leading to an open window,' Pembridge said sarcastically, but without malice. Toby sensed she was interested in his hunch, and seconds later she joined him to scour the skirting boards and plug sockets. But there was nothing there; no droplet of blood that might suggest

Harrington had been attacked elsewhere and staggered back to his desk to die.

'We should still get them to test this corridor for blood,' Toby said as they returned to the room. Frustrated but undeterred, he crossed to the desk and peered at the papers arranged on it. They were the pages of a contract Harrington must have been reviewing, several sheets dotted with crossings-out, indecipherable annotations and angry question marks.

'Do you think he was disturbed while working on this?' he asked.

Pembridge nodded. 'Looks like it. He's only marked up the first few pages from left to right.'

'What is it?'

'An agreement with a roofing contractor for some works on one of their properties. Nothing seemed very significant.'

Friedel peered at the neatly-arranged pages, noticing the address of the proposed works.

'The place is a hikers' rest stop in the woods,' he said, frowning. 'A weird building for them to own, don't you think?'

He took out his phone and snapped a couple of pictures. He was aware of Pembridge's gaze on him, sensing how uncomfortable she was at him apparently critiquing her work.

'Who do you think disturbed him?' he asked, trying to change the subject.

She shrugged. 'The only people here were the two care workers working the night shift, and all the residents.'

'Could either of the women have done it?' The case notes advised that the two workers were a Stephanie Glebe and a Marie Derbyshire.

Pembridge shook her head. 'Can't rule it out, but I don't think so.'

'An inmate?'

'You make it sound like a prison.'

'Isn't it?' he quipped.

'I suppose so,' Pembridge replied, a momentary sadness in her voice. 'But no, they're all either too old and infirm or too lacking in marbles, or both. It's like a scene from *The Walking Dead* downstairs.'

'So if it was someone else... who?'

'I haven't spoken to the dead man's business partner yet. He's proving somewhat elusive.'

Toby nodded again. 'Harrington's wife called McKenzie earlier, and said something about dubious business dealings. She tried to retract it, but it sounded like she was worried about some scandal coming out.'

'Or maybe it was a professional hit, and she arranged it.'

'We should talk to her again.'

Pembridge nodded. Toby looked around the room once more, hoping for a flash of inspiration. He prayed they wouldn't have to trawl through every document that was piled on or filed inside the cabinets; hopefully they could palm that off onto a forensic accountant somewhere. Some of the stacked papers looked decades old, the paper as yellow and fragile as parchment. Harrington was clearly a hoarder. The sort of person who might have secret places to store valuable possessions.

A flash of inspiration.

Toby pointed at the highborn gent depicted on the portrait. 'Am I supposed to recognise him?'

'Apparently he used to own the place.'

Toby approached the painting, feeling along its sides.

'Why, what are you thinking?' Pembridge asked.

'Another hunch,' he replied, hoisting the picture upwards and away from the wall. Behind it was a small black safe with a keypad.

'Well, what about that,' whispered Pembridge approvingly.

The cinnamon taste of triumph. Toby tried to open the safe, unsurprised to find it locked. A sudden shadow fell across the exposed wall, and he turned to see Greg looming in the doorway, carrying two distinctly un-steaming mugs. The care worker didn't say anything, standing sulkily on the other side of the crime scene tape.

'Thanks, Greg,' said Toby. 'Leave them there on the floor, please. We'll get them in a minute.'

The man stooped, depositing the cups on the carpet as instructed. Somehow he managed to make even that movement appear resentful.

'I wonder if Harrington is the type of person who writes his passwords in a little notebook in his desk,' mused Pembridge hopefully.

'Or maybe Braithwaite knows the combination. Like you said, I should talk to him next.'

'Don't you mean "we"?' Pembridge replied, raising an eyebrow.

'Nope. Because I want you to find out where this address is.' He pointed at the contract on the desk. 'It might be nothing, but we need every lead we can get.'

Pembridge looked put out.

Here comes the hard part, Toby thought. He could pull rank on her, or he could play it gently. Pembridge had done a good job so far – she was clearly a conscientious detective, and there was no point antagonising her. 'Listen,' he said, holding her gaze. 'I'm not here to undermine you. We're a team, okay? I'm just suggesting what I think we should do. If you think it's a stupid idea, we can take a different approach.'

Pembridge stared back at him for a moment, defiance glimmering in her eyes. Then she shook her head. 'No, you're right. I'm annoyed I missed it, that's all.'

Toby nodded, relieved. He turned to Greg, who was

hovering at the doorway once again, like some persistent crime scene groupie. Maybe he *did* watch *CSI*. 'Greg, do you know where we can find Ian Braithwaite?'

The man shrunk backwards, seeming horrified by the question. 'He doesn't talk to minions like us,' he grunted. 'You'd have to call his assistant, at head office.'

'Do you have the number?' Toby persisted, deploying his most disarming smile. 'Or better yet, the address?' Greg sighed, nodding. 'Terrific – if you could write them both down here, we'll leave you to enjoy your day.'

Toby kept the smile fixed firmly in place as he handed Greg his notepad and pen.

17

GREG TAPSON

(CARE WORKER, BROOKHAVEN HALL)

B loody pigs, treating him like a bloody bellboy. And now they were going to get him in trouble with one of the bossmen – the *only* bossman, in fact, after the other one got filled in by someone right here in the care home! Greg couldn't afford trouble with his employer. He couldn't afford to lose *this* job, not again; not with another babby on the way, not with a criminal record that normally precluded him from applying for anything better than cash-in-hand manual labour. Thankfully Harrington and Braithwaite didn't seem to be too hot on paperwork, or checking references.

What to do, Greg? If the police turned up at head office asking questions, his superiors might trace it back to him, and then he'd be right in the shit. He'd heard the rumours, that Braithwaite was the real brains of the operation, letting Harrington do all the shouting and fronting things up while the little weasel pulled the strings in the background. For all Harrington's bluster, Greg had been reliably informed that Braithwaite was the one to be truly feared. The last time Braithwaite came to Brookhaven in person he apparently hadn't said a word to any of the staff, then later told the manager to fire one of the employees because he didn't like their shoes.

Greg had learned, the hard way, that brushes with authority rarely worked out well for him. Back in school it had been the teachers, pissed off that he skived their lessons to spend time smoking and copping off with the girls who fancied him because he looked older than the other boys, and could get served in the off-licence. Later it was the plod themselves, when he'd grown up and gotten involved in more than just illicitly buying bottles of 20/20 or Diamond White cider. Either way, he never seemed to be able to outwit the people who wanted to rein him in. Those bastards were always one step ahead, as though he had the word 'troublemaker' tattooed permanently across his forehead.

That was why he was trying to straighten himself out. And he really was trying. He'd met a nice woman who didn't mind looking after his other kids every second weekend. He'd wangled this job. Now, just when his life had been going all right, this whole business with the murder had bloody happened.

He sometimes felt like he wasn't cut out for their world. Whenever he played by the rules, he seemed to lose. Perhaps that was why he was so fascinated by what had happened to John Harrington, and by the fact that such an audacious crime had been perpetrated right here inside Brookhaven. It made him feel good, almost invigorated, to see a big shot like Harrington knocked off his perch. Harrington had all the money in the world, more than Greg could even imagine; but it hadn't saved him, not when it came down to it. Not when someone had decided to stick a knife in his belly.

That was what Marie had told him had happened to the rich bastard. The nosey old bag had been working the night shift with Stephanie, and the young lass had found the body herself, so Greg had no reason to doubt Marie's version of events. Still, he was looking forward to his next shift with Stephanie, so he could grill her directly, get all the juicy details himself. He'd better be careful, though – he didn't want to accidentally blurt out any specifics in front of the filth. They'd see that big *troublemaker* tattoo and before he knew it, he'd be accused of the murder himself, used as a patsy by someone cleverer than he was. Back in chokey, unable to see his kids.

Tracy had already tried every trick she could think of to stop the pair of them from seeing him. And he knew that bitch had already tried to poison them against their new, as yet unborn sibling. It had made his insides curdle when Alfie had said *yeah but she won't be our* real *sister, will she?* He'd snapped at him about that, made him cry, and felt like garbage afterwards.

It was Tracy's fault. He hadn't meant it to work out this way, different kids with different mothers, all that rubbish. He'd tried to be a good dad. And he still saw the boys, despite that bitch always cancelling and rearranging, doing everything she could to mess him about. He still paid his child maintenance, even though he only earned a pittance at this dump.

He could feel himself getting angry as he wiped down the surfaces in the kitchen, thinking again about the blood he was going to have to clean up later, not that he planned to do a particularly thorough job. The coppers should damn well do it themselves. He watched through the window as their unmarked cars pulled away. Probably on their way to head office, to drop him in it, just like he feared. *Right in the shit.*

'Sod it,' he snarled, throwing the dirty rag in the sink and taking out his mobile phone. 'This is above my bloody pay grade.' It was time to make this Rebecca's problem. Sadly that meant talking to the care home manager, his immediate boss. He hated the fat, patronising cow; hated how she dyed her hair pink even though she was easily over forty, hated how she insisted on being called 'Bex', hated how she acted like she was better than him even though she lived alone with God knew how many cats.

But hey, needs must.

He jabbed at the screen, scrolling through to Rebecca's number.

18

BEX CATTERALL

(GENERAL MANAGER, BROOKHAVEN HALL)

B ex wandered along the aisle, making a point of grumbling loudly as she squeezed between the two cages that had been left unattended right in the middle of it. The supermarket was really letting its standards drop. Reaching the pet food section, she stooped to inspect the label of a new brand of cat food, one she hadn't seen before, promising tastier cuts of natural ingredients without the added sugars or filler, using entirely grain-free recipes. Apparently these succulent chunks were accompanied by sumptuous gravy, cooked with care for the preservation of taste. She could almost feel her own mouth watering.

Pity it costs over a bloody pound a tin.

She grunted in irritation, hauling herself upright and looking guiltily at the cheaper varieties on the other shelves. Surely Hoggle, Jareth, Sarah, Lancelot, Ludo and Diddimus would forgive her? She felt they understood, on some atavistic level, that she was doing her best, despite her crappy job and its crappier pay. Yet somehow, throughout her life, Bex's best had never seemed to be good enough.

Trying to put the remorse out of her mind, she reached for a multipack of sickly-looking, jelly-encrusted chicken chunks. Then her phone started to ring. She put the cans down and withdrew the phone from her satchel, wincing when she saw Greg Tapson's number, wishing not for the first time that she'd never recruited the scruffy creep.

But hey, needs must.

'Hello?' she answered, as politely as she could muster.

'Hello, Rebec–' A sigh. '*Bex*. I'm sorry for ringing you on your day off. But some coppers have just been in again to look at the crime scene.'

'Oh. Well, that's to be expected I suppose. Don't worry, I'm sure you handled it very well.' The gormless prick couldn't manage his way out of a paper bag, but then what did she expect, with the wages that Harrington and Braithwaite paid? It was no wonder she had to rely on a team full of ex-cons and losers. That made her think again about her own paltry pay packet, which made her sad, and she hated feeling sad. Better head home to Hoggle and Jareth and the others as quickly as possible, get snuggled up with them in front of Netflix. Maybe pick up some ice cream. Her diet could always start again on Monday, after all.

'They wanted to talk to Mr Braithwaite,' Greg mumbled, 'so I ended up giving them the details for head office. I think they're on their way there now. I thought maybe... someone should let them know? You know, so they don't drop us in it, or anything.'

Us. A problem skilfully handed over to her. *Just when the day had been going quite well.* The icy hand of dread tickled her chest; she *hated* talking to head office. The place was full of egomaniacs and backstabbers, from the bitchy receptionists to the slimeball that worked as Executive Assistant to Mr Harrington and Mr Braithwaite. No one was as bad as the old men themselves, though. She had to travel there every few weeks to report the care home's stats in person, and it felt as if her employers took deliberate steps to make the meetings as hostile as possible. She imagined herself seated at the opposite end of the long desk in the board room, laughing nervously like she always did, the too-bright lights dazzling her and making her hot and sweaty and discombobulated.

'Okay,' she heard herself say, an unpleasant warmth spreading across her face. 'I'll... call them. Thanks for letting me know.'

Greg grunted a goodbye and hung up, sounding mightily relieved to have batted the issue into her court. Bastard. *But it's better to face your problems*, she reminded herself, *instead of letting them grow and fester*. Just like Doctor Zoltanfi said. *You've got to nip them in the bud, Rebecca*. Doctor Zoltanfi never remembered to call her Bex either.

Mouth puckering with distaste, she swallowed heavily and scrolled through to Giacomo's number. It rang once, twice, and she prayed for voicemail, a chance to pass the baton neatly to Giacomo, just as Greg had done to her. Her heart sank when the Italian answered.

'Hello?'

'Ahh, hi. Giacomo. I'm on my day off, but I've just had Greg Tapson on the phone.'

'Who is this?'

'Oh, sorry.' She could feel herself getting flustered already. 'It's Bex.'

'Who? Oh, right: Rebecca, from the care home.'

She sighed. 'Yes. I'm just calling to let you know that the police are apparently on their way to you. Two detectives have been to Brookhaven, asking for the head office address details. They're looking for Mr Braithwaite.'

The other end of the line was silent, apart from the sucking sound of a long, harassed breath. The inhalation was laced with exasperation, infused with an accusatory undertone. It seemed to say *I intend to hold this against you, Rebecca.*

'Thanks for the heads up,' Giacomo said eventually, and hung up.

Rebecca sighed with relief, aware that her face had turned the same bright red colour as the gaudily packaged cat food. She reached again for the cans, realising as she did so that her hands were shaking.

19

GIACOMO ESPOSITO

(EXECUTIVE ASSISTANT, HARRINGTON AND BRAITHWAITE PROPERTY GROUP)

'Yes, Yelena, you can send him up.' He'd been expecting two officers, but only one had arrived, not long after Rebecca's call. The useless lump had probably gotten confused.

'Okay,' replied the receptionist, sounding a little rattled by the arrival of the police at her place of work. Giacomo didn't blame her. He was more than a little shaken himself. He smoothed back his hair and checked his reflection in the mirror he kept in his desk drawer. Aside from a slight pallor, everything was as it should be: black locks slicked back, eyebrows carefully plucked, handsome face devoid of blemishes and looking at least a decade younger than its forty-four years. But anxiety shifted behind that pristine veneer, like something hideous and hungry lurking beneath the surface of a crystalline pool.

He slid the drawer shut and extracted a gritty lump of chewed-up fingernails from his mouth, sprinkling them into the wastepaper bin beneath his desk. He knew biting his nails was a disgusting habit, particularly when he found himself surrounded by a circle of masticated remains at the end of a stressful workday. He smiled grimly as he imagined a ring of salt that some warlock had spread around a demon in order to entrap it. The place certainly did feel like a prison sometimes – but the *real* demon was the man he'd spoken to over the phone, minutes earlier. His one remaining boss. Ian Braithwaite seemed to be in an even more foul mood than usual, as though trying to compensate for John Harrington's death by being vicious enough for the pair of them.

After the call from the care home manager, Giacomo had phoned Braithwaite immediately. The conversation had gone about as well as the executive assistant had expected.

'Didn't I say never to call me when I'm here?' Braithwaite had sibilated, his voice as snakelike and menacing as always.

'I know, Mr Braithwaite, but it's the *police*. They've been to Brookhaven again, and now they're coming here to look for you.'

'So do your job and fob them off. Isn't that what I pay you for? Or do I need to reconsider your employment status?'

How was someone working in these conditions supposed to stop biting their nails? 'Yes, sir,' he replied meekly.

The problem was that Giacomo knew too many of Harrington and Braithwaite's secrets. In theory this made him indispensable, unsackable... but it also meant that if he *really* wanted to get rid of him, Ian Braithwaite might decide to terminate Giacomo in more ways than contractually. Giacomo's knowledge of his employers' dealings meant he knew this was a very real possibility. Harrington and Braithwaite were men who had their fingers in a lot of pies, some of which were distinctly unsavoury.

He straightened his tie and adjusted his waistcoat, taking comfort from the immaculate gleam of his shoes as he rose and crossed from his corner desk to the door. The office's other two desks were much bigger than his, reinforcing his lowly status. They faced away from each other on opposite sides of the room, an illustration of just how poisonous the relationship between the company's two owners had become. Giacomo wondered if the atmosphere would improve now that one of the old curmudgeons had been bumped off. He sincerely doubted it. Not for the first time, he also wondered whether Ian Braithwaite was the one who'd arranged the bumping.

He glanced at Harrington's desk, grimacing at the mess. *Surely the police would ask questions about it.* Despite his hurried attempts to tidy it, the workstation was still a shambles of emptied files and scattered paperwork, looking as though someone had recently ransacked it – which was exactly what Giacomo had done, at his boss's request.

'Harrington had some incriminating photos of Eric Potter taken at the Cabin,' Braithwaite had explained, voice dripping with malevolence. 'Did you know about them?'

'No,' Giacomo had replied, truthfully. 'I promise.'

'I need you to find them. Check his desk, his files, everywhere. And don't put it past the bastard to have a trick drawer or secret compartment somewhere.'

But Giacomo's search thus far had proved fruitless, although he had unearthed an alarming stack of unpaid invoices and threatening reminders from various contractors. He started reordering some of the mess, knowing his efforts were futile. They were soon interrupted by a knock at the door, which he opened with his most disarming smile, finding himself confronted by a male officer in plain clothes. The man was maybe five years younger than Giacomo, and alarmingly white, with his skin and his hair almost the same ashen hue. He was holding up his ID, pre-empting Giacomo's challenge.

'Hello, Officer Friedel,' Giacomo said, as warmly as he could manage. 'Follow me, and we can talk in the boardroom. There are biscuits in there.' He added a conspiratorial wink, but the policeman didn't seem in the mood for pleasantries. Giacomo stepped out into the hallway, closing the door quickly behind him before the detective could peer inside.

'I'm here to see Mr Braithwaite,' Friedel said as he followed him along the corridor. 'Is he here?'

'I'm afraid Mr Braithwaite is taking a business trip, visiting some prospective clients.' Giacomo's smile felt as if two nails had been driven through his cheeks to hold it in place.

'When will he be back?'

'He's planning to spend the weekend in Bath, but I expect he'll be back in the office on Monday.' He had no idea why Bath popped into his head, but at least it gave him time to concoct a new cover story for the following week should Braithwaite want to continue to avoid the police. Although it also meant they might go and pester his employer at his house later, to confirm the story was true. That might land Giacomo in hot water... but what could he do about it? At least that would be better than them somehow tracing his boss to the Cabin. He almost shuddered at the thought.

'And is he contactable?' the detective pressed.

Giacomo opened the meeting room door, ushering his visitor inside and offering him a chair. The man didn't sit down, sauntering around the room instead, peering at the pictures on the walls. A few of them depicted successful building projects, but most were photographs of Harrington beaming at various awards ceremonies or meetings with politicians. In one photo, taken perhaps a decade ago, he was shaking hands with Eric Potter. Giacomo thought again about the *other* photographs, the ones Braithwaite had mentioned.

'I'm afraid Mr Braithwaite often switches his mobile phone off when he doesn't want to be disturbed,' Giacomo said regretfully, which was not a lie. 'It's likely I won't be able to speak with him until next week.' This was very much a lie, because Ian had ended their earlier conversation by demanding an update the moment the police had left.

'Then perhaps *you* can help us,' the policeman replied. Like

Giacomo, he spoke perfect English but with a non-British accent, in his case probably German, judging by his name. He mirrored Giacomo's smile, looking utterly insincere, and the Italian wondered for a moment if that was how he himself appeared to others: obsequious and sycophantic. He felt his own expression falter, straining to hold it in place, as though the two of them were engaged in a bizarre competition. 'As you've already observed, I'm Detective Inspector Friedel,' the detective continued. 'Your name is?'

'Giacomo Esposito,' he replied.

'And you're Mr Braithwaite's–'

'Executive assistant,' he interjected tersely, not wanting to hear himself described as a 'secretary' for the umpteenth time.

'Do you have any dealings with the care home yourself?'

'As part of my range of duties, I assist with the company's entire portfolio,' he said proudly. 'I therefore have dealings from time to time with all of the company's residential and nursing homes... but I assume you're talking about Brookhaven?'

'I am. Have you ever been there personally?'

Giacomo realised that Friedel had taken several steps towards him. He felt suddenly cornered, his Brooks Brothers tie tightening like a noose. 'I have,' he answered stiffly.

'And are you aware of the room that Mr Harrington liked to use as an office?'

'Why, er, why don't I get you a drink, and we'll sit down?' Giacomo asked, thinking longingly about the glass he'd left on his desk. He moved towards the water cooler in the room's opposite corner, pushing past his unwanted visitor. 'Or perhaps you'd like me to have Yelena bring up some coffee, or–'

'That won't be necessary, thank you,' interrupted the smiling policeman. He appeared determined not to allow Giacomo to get comfortable. 'I was asking about the office at Brookhaven.'

'Yes, I've been there. It's normally used by the care home manager.'

'Do you know why Harrington was there so late on Wednesday night?'

Giacomo poured himself a water and lowered himself resignedly into the nearest chair. 'I don't, I'm afraid. His death was such a shock to all of us.'

'Did he often work there, instead of here?'

'Only occasionally.' He didn't add that it was somewhere Harrington liked to flee to when even being in the same room as Braithwaite had become temporarily intolerable. Giacomo didn't blame him.

'Is there anything unusual about the office?' the detective continued. 'Anything... hidden?'

Giacomo frowned. 'I don't know what you mean.'

Friedel seemed to be mulling something over, chewing the corner of his lower lip. Then he leaned forwards, splaying his fingers on the long table and regarding Giacomo like a chess opponent. 'There's a safe, hidden behind a painting on the wall. Do you know what's inside it?'

A safe. Were there no lengths to which his bosses wouldn't go to conceal their affairs from each other?

'I haven't a clue, I'm afraid, detective.'

'Do you know the combination?' Friedel persisted.

'I didn't even know the safe existed.'

'Perhaps we can check Mr Harrington and Mr Braithwaite's desks,' Friedel said, still smiling, 'to see if the code is written down anywhere?'

'I'm sure a warrant would be required for that,' Giacomo replied evenly. He'd expected Friedel's smile to fade at that, but he was mistaken.

'That's okay,' the detective replied. Under the room's harsh lighting, his skin and hair reminded Giacomo of the colour of cocaine. *Fingers in a lot of pies.* 'I'll pick that up with Mr Braithwaite directly. Now, I know you mentioned that he might have it switched off, but how about giving us that mobile number anyway? It's been a while since I sat my National Investigators' Exam, but I'm pretty sure a warrant isn't required for that.'

Giacomo realised he was chewing his index fingernail, and snapped his hand away from his lips. 'Of course,' he replied, gagging slightly as the sliver of keratin slipped accidentally down his throat.

Mercifully, Friedel left soon after Giacomo had furnished him with the phone number. The Italian exhaled deeply, swiping a hand through his hair. He felt soiled by the encounter, in need of a shower. He returned to his desk, opening the drawer to check his reflection once again. Everything was still in place, yet somehow the façade looked damaged, crumbling like an ageing shop front. Slamming the drawer, he yanked open the one beneath it, removing the bottle he kept there and topping up the glass of 'water' he'd been sipping all morning. He knew that drinking vodka before lunch probably made him an archetypal alcoholic. *Working here, is it any fucking wonder?* He took out his E-cigarette, another habit in which he could freely indulge when he had the office to himself, and inhaled deeply as he expelled the scent of watermelon. As he vaped, he glanced at the little heap of fingernails alongside his keyboard; a fresh pile he had no memory of creating.

After another long drag on the E-cig, he called Ian Braithwaite again.

20

ELIRA NEZIRI

(SEX WORKER)

E lira tilted her head away from the old man. She couldn't help it; she felt sickened by his touch, by his grey little body and too-big Martian eyes. She, Irene and Camilla were seated in a row, and he was working his way from left to right like a cattle breeder weighing up a trio of prize heifers. The other two girls had already undergone the same humiliation; now it was Elira's turn to be inspected.

'Don't worry, I don't bite,' he intoned, gripping her chin and forcing her head firmly back towards him. His voice was like something slippery but dry, a serpent slithering amongst desiccated bones. 'But I do need to make sure you're up to the required standard. I have a VIP visiting later who is *very* particular.'

His eyes explored her body, seeming to swell even larger than their already bulbous state. She stayed as still as she could, knowing she couldn't afford to antagonise him, not with Ricky watching from the corner of the room. The pimp's stare was a different kind, one with a promise of violence barely concealed beneath it. He'd been ill with the flu, making him even more bad-tempered, and she could hear him sniffing every so often. It reminded her how cold the room was, the chair beneath her, her barely-concealed skin. She concentrated on trying not to shiver.

The old man's phone rang in his pocket, and he swore under his breath as he turned away to answer it. 'What happened?' he barked.

A male voice was audible through the speaker. 'One policeman turned up. He was asking questions about the office at Brookhaven, where John's corpse was found.'

She felt dread wrap itself around her, a pair of arms settling over her own, enfolding her cold flesh in their even icier embrace. Her world was one of bad people, terrible people; and now Ricky had brought them to this creepy house in the middle of nowhere, to this old man talking about dead bodies.

'What sort of questions?' snapped the old man.

Maybe it would be better if she died. She'd thought about it every day since she first set foot in the basement, when she saw the other women and realised too late, too late, what was really happening to her. But such ideas – like her emotions, like her ability to feel pain – were dulled now, made numb and abstract by codeine, and by the need for her mind to distance itself from its reality. For countless months, Elira had experienced life, and the endless conveyor belt of lascivious men it brought to her down those basement steps, through a curtain of dense fog.

'Why he was there so late, whether he worked there often,' replied the voice on the phone.

'And you told him you didn't know?'

Her memories, too, were becoming blurred and indistinct. Her childhood in Albania, cared for mainly by her grandmother, whose face looked like a gnarled tree. The stories the old lady used to tell her, reading from a dusty book about dragons and giants and mermaids. The day her father didn't return from work. Her mother crying. The first time she had learned about the idea of a 'debt', and understood that it could be a truly terrible thing.

Like being in chains, her mother had said.

'Of course,' replied the voice. 'But there's more: they've found a safe in there, behind the painting. The detective wanted to search both of your desks for the code.'

'A safe?' snapped the old man. 'The sneaky bastard...'

Now she had a debt of her own, or at least that's what Ricky had told her, to begin with. She had to fuck this man, that man, to pay off what she owed Ricky for smuggling her into the country. Now he rarely even bothered mentioning the debt to try to justify what was happening to her. There was no justification needed anymore. It was simply her life.

It turned out her belief that the UK would provide her with a better existence, an escape from blood feuds and suffering, was like another of her *gjyshja*'s fairy tales.

'Don't worry,' said the voice, sounding unnerved by the old man's rising temper. 'I told him he'd have to come back with a warrant.'

The room's chill air reminded her suddenly of the lorry that had first brought her here, back when she'd believed Ricky was a good man, someone trying to help her. There had been other people with her, other teenagers, entire families of illegal migrants and refugees. A young boy, almost a baby really, curled up on the floor.

'And *do* you know the code?'

It had been so cold that by the time they'd arrived, he was dead.

'I didn't know about the safe, Mr Braithwaite, I promise.'

The old man glanced suddenly over his shoulder at her, perhaps worried she'd overheard his name. Elira knew she wouldn't be able to do anything with it anyway. People of her kind were invisible, unwanted. Voiceless. Illegal immigrants like Elira might as well have been ghosts.

She stared listlessly at the ground as though not paying any attention at all.

'Good,' said the old man, perhaps simultaneously addressing her and the man on the phone. 'I need to know what Harrington was keeping in the safe, before the police find out. It might be where he was keeping the photos.'

A pause on the other end of the line. Then, with reluctance, 'What do you want me to do?' The man had an accent, possibly Italian. She wondered if he was in the same position she was: forced into a life of servitude, of having monsters like Ricky or this vile Mr Braithwaite controlling their every move.

'Search John's desk for the code,' the old man retorted impatiently. 'Like the policeman suggested.'

'But... what if I don't find it?'

Or maybe the man on the phone was just another monster himself.

'I don't know, go to Brookhaven yourself and search there. Pry it open with your bare hands.' The old man's voice rose to a reptilian growl. 'I pay you to be my assistant, so fucking *assist* me!'

He hung up and turned back towards her, face reddened, the vein at his temple pulsing dangerously. She shrank from his anger, thinking he might be about to hit her. Instead, he addressed Ricky.

'Okay, I'll take these last two. The first one doesn't do it for me, I'm afraid – it's the tattoos.'

Elira felt her heart simultaneously sink and soar, her stomach lurching as it flooded with a hellish brew of guilt and relief, dread and concern. She and Irene would be forced to stay here, to do whatever this hateful old man wanted for the rest of the evening. But at least they were away from Ricky's oppressive surveillance for a little while. And at least they hadn't been rejected like poor Camilla, who would be bundled back into the van and driven back to 'the House', as they all called it.

Camilla's olive skin was adorned with swirls and symbols, skulls and roses and insignia that she had proudly told Elira were her own design. Camilla had been helping Elira with her English; like most of the girls who lived at the House, Camilla was British. Elira had been surprised that not everyone was in the same position as her, brought there from overseas and held under false pretences, without a passport or even a bank account. It seemed this was a stereotype sustained to hide an even more unpalatable truth: it often wasn't only foreigners, tricked and trafficked, that men like Ricky preyed upon.

She watched as the pimp accepted some cash from the old man, and then gripped Camilla by the elbow, propelling her out of the chair and into a standing position. Ricky was short and wiry, almost comically so, resembling a child when he stood next to his taller clients. But his constant visits to the gym made him deceptively strong and lean. Elira had learned this in her first twenty-four hours in the House, when she'd tried to escape from him and been left with a black eye and a broken collarbone.

The money she'd been unable to earn while she healed had been added to her debt, of course.

Like being in chains.

'I'll be back to pick you up in the morning,' he rasped, his aggressive Cockney twang made phlegmy and guttural by his lurgy-ridden lungs. His eyes, red-rimmed and sickly, burned threats into theirs. 'Do whatever you're told, and don't cause any problems.'

He marched Camilla out of the room. Elira wondered whether he'd beat her in the van, or wait until they were back at the House. The trees outside the window seemed to burn red with outrage. Elira looked at them, thinking about the woodland that completely encircled the cottage, obscuring the dirt track that had led them to it. She wished her and Irene could disappear amongst those boughs, like Hansel and Gretel.

More fairy stories. The trees, swaying and rustling with the allure of their promised sanctuary, might as well have been a million miles away.

21

RICKY COX

(HUMAN TRAFFICKER AND PIMP)

Ricky shifted his grip from the bitch's arm to her hair, and shoved her hard into the back of the van. He glanced at the burly security guard on the door, who had eyed him aggressively when Ricky had first arrived at the house. Sometimes men like that fancied themselves as heroes, especially if they'd read too many Jack Reacher novels. But the big lump continued to stand idly in the porch, leaning against the wall. He didn't even bother to meet Ricky's gaze, seeming more interested in the piece of chewing gum he was rolling around in his wide jaws. Evidently this chump was unlikely to leap to a whore's defence.

Besides, it wasn't Ricky's fault he was angry. Camilla had disgraced him, making him look like some second-rate flesh peddler. He slammed the van's rear doors, disgusted by the sight of her. Then he changed his mind, unable to help himself, and climbed inside instead.

'No, please, Ricky, I didn't—'

She soon shut her mouth when he punched her in the face. He knew straight away he'd been too rough, when her eyes rolled back and she sagged against the wall, gurgling blood. He might even have chipped one of her teeth. Well, she could pay for the dental work. It was her fault, hers and this fucking flu, messing with his head so much he could hardly concentrate.

'Keep your trap shut, you gobby cow, or there's more of that for you,' he snarled from inside the balloon of snot that had replaced his head. 'And don't think you can sweet-talk me like you normally do. That's a valuable new customer, and you've just pissed him right off with your fucking tramp stamps.'

He slammed the doors closed and circled around the van to the driver's side, breathing through his mouth because his nose was too bunged up. This time the goon gave him a pointed stare, still chewing his gum like a naughty schoolboy. He probably thought it made him look tough. *Prick*.

Still, thanks to the virus that riddled his system, Ricky was in absolutely no position to antagonise the lummox. He averted his eyes as he hoisted himself into the driver's seat, even that effort leaving him momentarily exhausted. *What a bloody life.* Camilla evidently didn't remember that she owed him everything. He'd saved her from herself, and from that animal Liam, who used to beat her every day, not to mention having her so hooked on the Charlie that her nose had probably been about to fall off. Maybe Ricky should sell her back to him, teach the ungrateful bitch a lesson. She was pushing thirty now, nearly over the hill. Perhaps Ricky's soft spot for her was clouding his judgement.

No room for sentimentality in this game.

He took out the cash Braithwaite had given him and counted it quickly to cheer himself up. Rich customers always paid over the odds; Ricky wasn't sure if they were daft, or just didn't care. A nice problem to have, he supposed. Jealousy burned in his veins, and he jammed the van into reverse and backed up aggressively, hauling the vehicle in a sharp arc to face the overgrown path that led back through the trees. There was a clattering noise in the back, probably the sound of Camilla being sent flying by the sudden turn. There were seats in there, along both sides, but no belts. *What did she expect, a fucking limousine?*

He lowered the window and spat out a mouthful of mucus as he set off. Gravel crunched under his tyres, but soon the grit thinned out, replaced by a rough dirt track through the woods. This place, this 'Cabin', really was well-hidden. Maybe Braithwaite wasn't so daft after all. Like the old creep had said: the girls weren't for him, they were for clients of his own, who were presumably even richer, even dafter. Maybe Ricky was the one getting ripped off.

He felt his fingers tighten around the steering wheel, a growing urge to tear it off and toss it into the woods. He knew he had 'anger issues'; but who wouldn't, in his situation? When you were small everyone regarded you as easy prey, a joke. You had to get on the front foot, show them you meant business. If that got you a reputation as a bit of a psycho, well, that wasn't a bad thing.

The path curved to the left, and the van rattled along it, the strange atmosphere inside the forest seeming to deaden the jolts and bounces that were probably wrecking the vehicle's suspension. The trees formed a thick canopy overhead, the afternoon sunlight only filtering through in glittering fragments as though the branches were studded with gold. Ricky felt for a moment as if he was inside a dream. Maybe he was. His life seemed that way sometimes, like something not quite real. He existed at right angles to normal people, their realities only intersecting when they wanted him to satisfy their needs. He was a creature summoned from a different dimension, a dark place that everyone wanted to pretend didn't exist, one full of pimps and whores and violence.

Sometimes he thought about killing all of those bitches. Just going down into the basement with a gun and putting a bullet in each of their heads. Then maybe his own. He knew someone who could get him a pistol. It would be so easy. Easier than this constant pressure, a life like an endless migraine, made even worse by this *fucking, fucking flu!*

He was too lost in his dark thoughts to bother looking to the left as the van emerged onto the road. The vehicle burst through an overgrown crop of raspberry bushes that served as an ideal camouflage, making the trail almost impossible to discern if you didn't know where to look. This was a pity, because at that moment a car was hurtling towards those same raspberry bushes, its driver entirely unaware of the dirt track or that a grubby transit van was about to pull out directly in front of him.

22

_____

CAMILLA SANTOS

(SEX WORKER)

For a moment, Camilla had thought she was going to die. The terror did not come at the point when Ricky, that bastard, had hit her so hard she was sure he'd broken her nose. It did not come even when he'd driven like such a maniac she'd been flung into the opposite wall and smashed her nose again, leaving a bloody imprint on the van's interior. Sitting in the back of the vehicle as they bumped along, knowing the numbness in her face would soon give way to pain, she'd watched the blood dripping slowly, thickly, down to the floor between her feet. Like her life, ebbing away. She knew she probably needed to go to hospital, but there was no way Ricky would take her in a million years. At least there were painkillers back at the House.

No, the fear for her life came along with the almighty impact, not a crash but a _crunch_, when the van and her temporary prison cell were propelled suddenly forwards, this time not launching her into the far wall but pressing her into her seat as the vehicle yawed sideways, cracking her skull against the metal. _That_ pain came immediately, as if an axe had been driven into the back of her head. Even as the vehicle came to rest, tilted at a 45-degree angle both downwards and to the left, the space around her continued to spin, spots of brightness and agony exploding in the dim light around her like someone was setting off fireworks on her retinas.

For a while, she thought she would pass out, but the sound of a horn blaring insistently outside seemed to demand that she stayed awake, reminding her she'd been in a crash. *You need to get out*, it shrieked. *Ricky might be dead, and the van might be about to catch fire, and you'll be trapped inside and roasted alive.* She staggered to her feet, feeling like she was in one of those haunted houses where the floors and perspectives are distorted. She moved first towards the driver's end of the van, where a little latticed grille allowed light to filter into the cargo area. *Such precious cargo*, she thought, *so delicately handled.* She snorted a laugh, a bright bubble of blood inflating from one nostril, summoning fresh blitzkriegs of pain as it burst. Her whole head was aching now, like a shattered vase glued clumsily back together.

'Ricky?' she called. He didn't answer. She realised the sound of the horn was coming from the van itself, not outside. 'Ricky, are you all right?' Still nothing. 'I... I think I need an ambulance,' she slurred, sagging to her haunches as the van seemed to tilt again. Maybe it had, and it was rolling down the side of a steep hill, and the moment of her death had merely been delayed. Tumbling down a ravine would be the perfect final flourish for the pitiless narrative God had woven for her.

The spinning stabilised. She tried to get up on her tiptoes so she could peer through the tiny window, wondering if she'd see Ricky lying there unconscious, or with his head jutting through a shattered windscreen, or his face smashed to bits against the steering wheel. She wondered how she'd feel if he were dead. But despite straining and squinting she couldn't see much of anything, except that the windscreen was patterned with a filigree of cracks, and that beyond it was a blur of green, as though the van had come to rest face down in a field.

At least it wasn't teetering on the edge of a cliff.

She turned and stumbled towards the van's rear doors, having to hunker down to scramble up the brief but sharp climb towards them, almost falling backwards as another wave of dizziness crashed through her. She reached the doors, fumbling at the handles, knowing Ricky had locked her in. At least she could hold on to them for purchase with one hand while she hammered on the metal with the other.

'Help... please... I'm trapped in here...'

The sound of the horn might as well have been all that remained in the world. Its obstinate din, its very *wrongness*, told her no one was coming to help. She was alone, trapped in a wrecked vehicle. Even if she did get out, without Ricky she'd have nowhere to go, no way of making any money. Turning out renegade would only attract the other pimps. Like a pack of hyenas they'd encircle her, and she'd be forced to pick a favourite, a new 'daddy', unless she wanted to be beaten senseless and dumped in an alleyway.

'Please,' she sobbed, more to God than to anyone outside.

The doors were wrenched suddenly open and the handle torn from her grasp. This yanked her forwards, and she fell against the edge of the van's up-jutting floor like a stricken climber clinging to a rocky outcrop. The sun drove its rays into her throbbing, blood-misted eyes, and she blinked as she tried to look upwards. 'Ricky?' she rasped into the merciless light.

As the glare faded, she could see an enormous, bald man staring down at her, his eyes widened in a sort of muted surprise. *Nothing shocks me anymore*, the eyes seemed to say, *but you just came very close.*

'Jesus,' he said in a deep, melancholic rumble. 'Are you okay?' He offered her one massive hand. She gripped the calloused paw and hauled herself up and out of the van, sagging onto the dirt beyond. A glance behind her told her that the vehicle had been forced into a ditch by the roadside. Ahead, a black 4x4 had pulled up next to the shallow trench, its driver door hanging open, front bumper severely dented.

'I thought you said there was no one with you?' the big man said, turning ponderously, as if his body was too large to move all at once and he had to rotate one limb at a time. Behind him she could see Ricky, his own face bloodied, a deep cut visible on the bridge of his nose. He'd been hurt in the crash, but not as badly as she was. The pimp didn't reply, his breath wheezing in and out in the flu-choked snuffle she'd become accustomed to over the last few days.

'I asked you a question,' the big man insisted, in a voice that suggested he was used to such questions being answered. His back was to her, impossibly wide, as if his torso had been split in half and an extra one inserted in between the separated parts. He was tall as well as broad, standing at least six feet six inches, maybe the largest human she'd ever seen in the flesh. Ricky, almost entirely obscured by the stranger's bulk, squirmed and fidgeted, one hand pressed against the wound between his eyes. Blood oozed out from beneath his fingers like gory tears.

'Look, I don't want any trouble,' Ricky snivelled. 'We'll just get on our way... I won't even press charges or nuffink.'

'Unless by "on your way" you mean the hospital, you aren't going anywhere,' the leviathan growled. 'Your friend here looks pretty banged up.'

Ricky was silent once again. His face was contorting, oscillating rapidly between different expressions: fury, frustration, outrage, disbelief. All the stages of grief, crammed into a few split seconds. Eventually he emitted a sort of petulant grunt, and turned away from them as though he might be about to run off crying along the embankment.

The big man swivelled towards her. 'I'm Harry,' he said, offering her his hand once again and helping her to her feet. She stood woozily, leaning against the van, wondering if this friendly giant was some sort of concussion-induced hallucination. 'I'm not going to ask you for any specifics, because I know these things are complicated. But I also know people don't keep their friends locked in the back of a van when there's an empty passenger seat next to them. So I need you to nod, or shake your head, when I ask you three questions. The first one is: did you understand what I just said?'

She nodded slowly, feeling her head might fall to pieces if she did it too vigorously.

'Good. Are you being kept in that van against your will?'

Was this it? God's intervention, her chance to escape? This strange man was a policeman maybe, some sort of undercover operative. Perhaps that was why he'd driven them off the road.

Or perhaps he was another scumbag, one who could beat her even more brutally than Ricky. She stared in sudden horror at his massive hands, imagining the damage they could do even without being clenched into fists. She'd trusted Ricky, once. And Liam before him. And they'd taught her that men were all the same.

She shook her head.

The man closed his eyes for a moment, exhaling sadly, like someone who had received a piece of disappointing news. 'Okay,' he said. 'Now I have one more question, and I want you to think really carefully before you answer it. Because if you don't tell the truth, I think you'll regret it. I know it's hard to believe someone who... who looks like me. But I can help you, if you trust me.'

Behind the man – Harry – she could see Ricky pacing in

agitation. Perhaps he was about to insist that the newcomer stopped talking to her and dealt with him instead. But he was too frightened; Harry weighed at least twice as much as he did. Eventually the pimp disappeared from view, darting towards the front of the van. Camilla heard the door opening, and wondered if he was going to try to drive the vehicle straight up and out of the ditch.

'Okay,' Harry continued. 'I can see there aren't any seatbelts back there, so you must have been knocked about pretty badly when we collided. But I wasn't driving very fast, and I'm uninjured, and so is your "friend", apart from that cut on his nose. So my question is this: were your injuries all caused by the crash?'

Camilla closed her eyes. A great weight seemed to have gathered inside her head, and not only because of the wounds she'd sustained. It was as though all her life, the decade of drugs and sex and abuse she'd somehow lived through – not *survived*, not really, because that suggested a battle, a brave struggle that she'd endured and won, when in reality all she'd done was somehow woken up each day, finding herself still not yet dead – had coalesced into a single knot of pain, pulsing in between her eyes. A lump of anguish that this person was offering, like a cranial surgeon, to remove for her.

But the price he demanded was a great one indeed. A toll that Ricky would not hesitate to exact upon her body if it backfired. Harry wanted *trust*. This meant he was asking her to betray the person that owned her.

She didn't know if she had any trust left to give away.

'Why... are you helping me?' she croaked.

'I like your tattoos,' Harry said, smiling kindly.

She found herself smiling back. Then she closed her eyes, and swallowed, and shook her head. *No, they weren't all caused by the crash.*

I need your help.

At that moment, Ricky appeared behind her benefactor, teeth bared like a demon, swinging the hammer with all the strength in his lithe, compact body.

23

HARRY TORRANCE

(FORMER SAS TROOPER)

The attempt at a sneak attack hadn't bothered Harry too much; it was entirely predictable, which was why he'd predicted it, and had been poised to effortlessly turn and dodge and send the blow arcing wildly through empty air.

Even the state of the poor girl, emaciated and battered, hadn't been enough to really incense him. He'd seen it before, more times than he wanted to count: his brain had become desensitised to the atrocities inflicted on females by men in the name of religion, or race, or profit, or their own sexual inadequacies.

No, it was the lying that had flipped his long-dormant switch. The callousness with which the little snot rag had claimed that he'd been driving alone, when for all he knew the woman was dead in the back of the van, or crying out for help with a broken back.

The weight of the hammer dragged Harry's assailant after it, leaving him wide open, his scrawny body exposed like an anatomy diagram. In the end Harry waited until he straightened up, and smashed a massive right cross into his face. The bones of the little man's cheeks and eye sockets collapsed like a mask made out of papier mâché.

The girl screamed, as Harry knew she would, while her abuser crumpled to the floor like a discarded marionette. Harry ignored her for the time being, concentrating on working efficiently. He launched the hammer into the trees, hurling it like an Olympian, before he scooped up its owner's body as if it was a sack of garden clippings. The man – Ricky, she'd called him – was still alive, breath coming in liquid burbles through the layer of shattered viscera. He'd survive with medical attention, but Harry hadn't decided yet whether he was going to bother to summon any. He wasn't worried about Ricky talking to the authorities; Ricky wouldn't be doing much except sucking smoothies through a straw for weeks. Harry just didn't know enough about him to determine whether he deserved a second chance.

He clambered carefully down into the ditch, where the van's passenger door hung open, as did the glovebox from which Ricky had grabbed the hammer. There was a set of knuckle dusters in there, which Harry pocketed before closing the compartment, wincing at the incessant din from the broken horn. He shut the passenger door, circled to the opposite side, and opened the driver's door to deposit Ricky on the seat. The unconscious man slumped forwards onto the steering wheel, his pulped face helpfully oozing blood onto it. Now he looked exactly like someone who'd been involved in a bad car accident.

Harry shut the door in the manner of someone slamming closed an offensive book.

He moved to the back of the van once again, where Camilla was now sitting on the grass. Closing the rear doors, he hunkered down to talk to her. 'I'm going to call an ambulance for him once we're away from here,' he said gently. 'Now come on – I'll take you to a hospital.'

She shook her head as firmly as she could manage, given her injuries.

'I'm assuming he hit you at least once, and you've also been in a car crash. You need medical attention.'

'No,' she said resolutely, her eyes blazing with defiance. They were big and brown, like the conkers Harry used to play with at school.

He sighed. 'Okay.' At least she hadn't completely clammed up, or gone into shock. 'What's your name?'

'Camilla,' she replied.

'Okay, Camilla. I've got somewhere we can go for now.' He held out that same oversized hand once again. She stared at it with an expression of terror and gratitude, the sort of look he'd seen many times before when people were liberated from extreme violence by extreme violence. It didn't matter whether you were in England or Afghanistan – human faces were universal, because humans were all much more similar than their wars and vendettas and hate speech tried to suggest.

'I know I'm asking you to trust me,' he continued. 'And there's no reason whatsoever for you to do that. And I won't stop you if you want to run off into these woods. But I think you should come with me instead. I'm a retired soldier, if that helps at all. I'm here in town because I owe someone a favour. I'll be leaving tomorrow, and I haven't got any plans, so if you're determined not to take my advice about seeing a doctor, I can at least help you find a place to stay.'

He saw her eyes move across him, taking him in. He knew he was a pretty horrific sight. Bald head that looked like a half-finished sculpture. Physique like a gorilla. One fist scraped and bloodied against a man's teeth.

'Okay, Harry,' she said. 'I suppose I haven't got any plans either.'

Her joke made him smile, and he realised how rarely this

happened. Not an expression forced for another's benefit, or deployed to show a vulnerable person he wasn't as aggressive and hostile as his appearance suggested; a genuine moment of pleasure, a mote of light against the world's dark background.

Together, they walked towards Harry's car.

Harry made an anonymous call to the emergency services while they drove towards the hotel, telling the call handler that he'd just driven past a stricken vehicle but had been unable to stop and assist. He found a space tucked into a corner of the Middlewich's optimistically large car park, where the damaged bumper would be hidden from view. Camilla was hesitant about following him up to his room; he could think of countless reasons why. But he sensed that she'd made a decision to trust him, and eventually she allowed herself to be led into the building.

They went in through the back entrance to avoid the reception staff, and thankfully didn't encounter anyone else on the stairs; people might leap to certain conclusions if they saw a half-ogre escorting a scantily-clad woman with a badly bruised face.

Harry's hotel room was dark, the dwindling autumnal sunshine shut out by the thick curtains that he'd closed as soon as he arrived, ensuring secrecy for any preparations he might need to undertake ahead of the evening's business. He assumed Camilla would appreciate the privacy.

'Er, come in,' he said awkwardly, moving first into the room and heading towards the tiny desk in the corner, sitting down on its even tinier chair. He was worried it might collapse beneath him, but wanted to make clear that the bed was a safe space for her and her alone.

'Don't worry, I can take the chair,' she said with a smile, but sagged suddenly against the door frame. He leapt to his feet and helped her to the bed, where she lay down, grimacing in discomfort as she lowered herself onto the mattress.

'I'm going to say one last time that you need to go to hospital,' he said, looking down at her. Her frame was unhealthily thin, but he couldn't help noticing how attractive she still was. It would be easy to get lost in the patterns and ciphers that adorned her copper-coloured skin. But Harry had learned a long time ago that you needed to be able to switch that part of your brain off; nothing good ever came of its whims and impulses. In Harry's case, if a woman was determined, things might happen. If they waited for Harry to make the first move, they'd be waiting a long time. It was just easier that way.

Camilla glanced to either side of her. 'Wow, you really are a soldier; this is a tidy room.'

'I only checked in a few hours ago. Haven't had a chance to mess it up yet.'

'Why did you say you were here?'

'I'll tell you later. For now, I want to know about you.' He lowered himself carefully into the absurdly small seat. 'Including who Ricky is, and why he had you stashed in the back of a van.'

She lifted her shoulders in a shrugging motion, like twigs rustling beneath thin sackcloth. 'He's my pimp. Me and seven other girls. We live in a basement and have sex with whoever he tells us to. In return he gives us drugs, and most of the time doesn't beat us up.'

Harry wasn't sure whether the substance of her life, or the matter-of-factness with which she summarised its horrors, was the more disturbing. She told him about the House, which she was pretty sure was in Macclesfield but couldn't be any more specific, and how three of them had been selected earlier that day for a 'special job'. How Ricky had stressed the need for them to make a good impression, to be on their best behaviour, as if they ever acted with anything other than absolute subservience. How the other two girls were still there, being prepared for an evening with a 'VIP'. Ricky had hit her because she was rejected by the old man who seemed to be in charge of the place.

'He didn't like my tattoos.'

'He's an idiot,' replied Harry, making her smile. 'What was his name?'

She told him she didn't know, nor did she know who the VIP was. Nor did she really care.

By the time Camilla had finished her stark and brutal story, the grim facts of her life laid bare like organs during an autopsy, Harry felt exhausted. He was silent while he reflected on what she'd told him.

'Well, you did ask,' she added apologetically.

He rose and crossed to the window, anger curling his hands into fists like the heads of two maces. 'I should have left him to die,' he growled.

'But you didn't,' she replied. 'Because you're a good man, I think.'

Don't be so sure, he thought. He forced his mind not to wander back to his service days, skating instead across his time as a wanderer, trying to find a niche for himself as a bouncer or a security guard or a bareknuckle fighter. Nothing seemed to fit him. After the Army, everything felt... purposeless.

'I won't let you down,' he promised as he turned to her. 'Tomorrow we'll get you to a shelter. And I'm going to go and get the other girls too. I've made this my business now. But first I have to finish my job. I was on my way to get some supplies for tonight, before you... appeared. And if you won't go to a hospital, I'll need dressings for your injuries. A change of clothes too. But I can't take the car now until after dark, otherwise people will see the damage, and maybe put two and two together. So I'll have to hike into town, which means I might be gone a while.'

She shrugged again. 'I'll be all right here,' she said. 'Just leave me the TV remote. And... maybe you could bring me back a sandwich?'

He nodded. 'No problem.'

She smiled, then frowned as her thoughts shifted. 'You keep talking about tonight. This "favour" you're here to do. Is it something bad?'

He considered the question, and shook his head. 'Probably not. Just settling a debt.' The teenager's face flickered in his mind, like it always did, a strobe he could never switch off. One of thousands of tragedies, hundreds of thousands, a flow of civilian bloodshed that two decades of war in the Middle East had done little to staunch.

Jones, his friend, had thought the boy was drawing a weapon, and responded with a bullet. It turned out the lad had been taking out a chocolate bar. He might even have been about to offer it to them. Against his better judgement, Harry had helped his comrade cover up the crime. Jones had two children and a sick mother to look after. Harry had felt trapped on a knife-edge, a chasm of toxic guilt on either side. But he'd felt like he'd made the better of two impossible choices.

Then Jones had confessed anyway, because he couldn't live with himself.

Harry's involvement landed him a dismissal, and would have got him a jail sentence but for the personal intervention of an MP. He still wasn't sure the leniency was deserved. Nonetheless, he'd stayed in contact with his benefactor, who at first seemed to be motivated solely by a patriotic belief that soldiers were heroes and that war was too complex for black-and-white legislation. Later, though, the politician started to ask

Harry for favours, in return for cash. Unsavoury, but nothing too deplorable. Threaten a rival here, ransack an office there. Harry didn't like it, but he'd needed the money. Gradually the requests had dried up, and Harry had rebuilt his life, repurposing it into something broken but enduring. Like an old piece of furniture.

Before the previous night, he hadn't heard from Eric Potter for five years. Then the old schemer had called him, sounding worried, desperate even. The MP had more or less begged for his help, offering him larger and larger amounts of money.

Harry had eventually told him he'd help him for free; but that after that, he didn't owe Potter anything ever again.

'Being in debt isn't much fun, is it?' said Camilla quietly. 'One of my friends says it's like being in chains.'

Harry looked at her for a few seconds, then nodded, unable to think of anything to say. He turned and left the room, hearing the door click shut behind him, locking automatically. He wondered if she'd still be there when he got back.

As he turned the corner of the corridor, a black man in a long, camel-coloured trench coat passed by him, looking momentarily startled before nodding politely. Harry nodded back. He was used to having that effect on people.

24

PATRICK ADEMOLA
(PRIVATE INVESTIGATOR)

The problem with being paranoid was that you learned to doubt even your own chronic suspicion. The bald behemoth he'd walked past certainly *could* be hired muscle, brought in by some key player in a murderous plot Patrick had yet to unravel. But he could also just be a bodybuilding fanatic, visiting his relatives up north. For now, the PI chose to add him to his lengthening mental list of loose ends, and concentrated on getting on with the evening's business.

He'd been down to the bar to try to relax his nerves, but some drunken, sunbed-orange woman roughly his own age had been shouting at her daughter over the phone, yelling obnoxiously at the staff when they asked her to lower her voice, so he'd decided to take his drink back to his room instead. He would be driving, so was only allowing himself a single bottle of Peroni; he knew the drink's impact on his mood would be largely psychological rather than alcoholic, and he didn't care, as long as it took the edge off. Multiple edges, to be more precise, each one pressing against his brain like a razor.

One of the blades was the usual fear of getting caught,

perhaps even arrested, having to spend a long and frustrating night waving around his Private Investigator licence and justifying his actions to the local police. They tended to struggle with the idea that a black man might be a detective as opposed to a burglar.

Another worry was the strong sense he was being drawn into something he'd rather stay out of. Hiding in the bushes, snapping photos of an unfaithful husband was one matter; messing with human traffickers was quite another. He wasn't sure yet how big Harrington's operation had been, how many people it involved... or how aggressively they would defend themselves from detection. But someone had murdered a high-profile businessman, savagely and very publicly. It could even be a rival enterprise, warning Harrington and his associates off their turf. It was not a hornet's nest Patrick wanted to stick his lockpick into.

A final, particularly barbed concern was that of guilt. He knew he was ripping Mrs Harrington off. From what he'd seen of the safe, he suspected he could crack it within minutes. But the risk he was taking deserved a premium, and it wasn't as if she was short of money, her fears about her husband's absent will aside. Patrick, on the other hand, was *always* short of money. Which meant he had no choice, not really. He'd have to swallow his reservations, along with the last sip of his lager, and get to work.

Night had fallen by the time he ventured out to the car. The unpredictable nature of his job meant he'd learned long ago that the best way not to be left without a vital tool was to keep them all in the boot of his vehicle. Yes, that meant his equipment was at greater risk of theft than if he kept it secured indoors, but aside from the camera which he usually kept around his neck, most of it wasn't very expensive or hard to replace. Tonight's task would probably require little more than the twisted piece of coat hanger he'd slid into his pocket. The snub-nosed revolver he'd slipped into the inside lining of his coat probably wouldn't be necessary, but it always made him feel a lot better.

As he set out towards Brookhaven, he spotted the 4x4 that had been deposited in the car park's far corner, presumably in an effort not to draw attention to it. In this case the attempt had backfired, because that sort of conduct attracted the scrutiny of men like Patrick, men whose abilities to spot anomalies and unusual behaviour had been honed over his decades with the West Midlands Police. Presented with a large, sparsely occupied parking area, ninety-nine per cent of motorists would park close to others, perhaps driven by an innate orderliness or, more likely, by the natural human desire to seek safety in numbers. *Everyone is parking in this section, so I should too; either no one gets clamped, or we all suffer together.* He squinted at the vehicle, and noticed significant damage to its front bumper, almost hidden by the wall and the darkness. Another loose end to file away, for now.

He found himself revisiting that loose end only minutes later, when he turned a corner of the tree-lined road to find an unexpected blaze of blue lights awaiting him. He tensed immediately, reducing his speed to an innocuous cruise, wondering what could be happening. As he approached, the lightshow resolved itself into an ambulance and two police cars congregated around a breakdown truck, which was assisting a white transit van sticking half out of a roadside ditch. He saw a stretcher being loaded into the back of the ambulance, its occupant looking little better than a heap of raw meat.

A nasty accident, perhaps. *A vehicle rear-ended and driven off the road, the culprit fleeing the scene and trying to hide their damaged bumper.*

Frowning, he kept going, updating the filing system in his head.

Brookhaven Hall

A Harrington and Braithwaite Care Home

Patrick parked his grubby, dark grey Volkswagen Golf – chosen precisely because it was one of the most common, unremarkable cars on Britain's roads – in the same spot as last time, a layby not far beyond the signpost. Then he hiked through the woods to the same spot he'd used for his ill-fated surveillance assignment two nights previously. There was no sign of any police cars, unmarked or otherwise, on the care home's grounds, but he wanted to be sure before he ventured inside. Through the binoculars, he observed the sprawling red brick building, hidden amongst the trees like something discarded and overgrown. *A lot like the people who lived inside it*, he thought. He remembered his long-deceased parents with a time-softened flicker of sadness.

He surveyed the windows, saw the same blonde woman that had discovered Harrington's body. She was doing something in the kitchen downstairs. In a surprisingly large number of murder investigations, the person or people who found the corpse and reported the crime ended up being the culprits, but he was positive that this wasn't the case here. The shock in the young woman's face, captured and preserved by his camera, had been far too real; and she'd had no way of knowing that, at the moment of her horrified scream, she'd had an audience.

Moments later, he saw the other care worker who'd been on duty that night – a plump middle-aged woman – walk past an upstairs window. It never paid to rule anything out, but she hardly fitted the profile of a cold-blooded killer either. No, this crime had been committed by an outsider, an interloper. Someone who'd been able to effortlessly and anonymously access the building even while Patrick had been watching it. He wished he knew how they'd done it – his own plan for gaining admission that night was a lot less subtle.

He shifted his binoculars to the office window, trying not to dwell on the idea that other pairs of eyes might also be watching the premises, the eyes of individuals or organisations who were perfectly happy to stab people to death in their own workplaces. The bloody smear had been cleaned from the window, but an aura of violence still clung to the room, like the residue left by some intruding vermin. The light inside was switched off so he couldn't see much beyond the glass, but several minutes of patient observation discerned no movement. Apparently the police had clocked off for the night.

Unless they've been summoned to the crashed van, and will be coming back later. Better hurry up.

He walked back through the trees to his car, not wanting to be spotted and mistaken for some lunatic emerging from the bushes, and drove onto the car park. Approaching the front entrance and pressing the buzzer, he applied a friendly smile like it was a cheap coat of paint. The older woman, not the blonde one, appeared from a side door wearing a hassled-looking frown.

'The other detective said you wouldn't be back until tomorrow,' she grumbled irritably as she opened the front door. Patrick smiled to himself, leaving the fake police ID he'd been about to produce in his pocket. Sometimes his trench coat did the job all by itself. He supposed he had Columbo to thank.

'I'm very sorry, ma'am,' he said. 'I'm an outside specialist they've brought in, and I've arrived earlier than anticipated. I was hoping to take a look at the scene tonight, rather than waiting for the morning.'

The woman grunted crossly. 'Suit yourself, but we've already bloody cleaned it, twice actually because Greg did such a crap job of it the first time, so don't go complaining that we've destroyed any evidence, because your friend said it was okay. I can't bloody believe we have to do it ourselves, to be honest, mopping up blood like a scene from a film...' Her muttered complaints continued as she turned and headed towards the stairs, and he inferred that he was being invited to follow her. She opened the security gate and they passed through it onto the staircase, and Patrick waited while she turned to close it behind them, glancing down a corridor that led away from the main hallway. His heart lurched when he saw an old woman standing there, almost silhouetted in the dim light, her head tilted at a sideways angle like someone who'd fallen asleep standing up.

'Mrs Vickers give you a fright, did she?' chuckled his guide. 'I'd have thought you coppers would have seen much worse. Don't worry, they're all harmless really – just bloody bonkers. You get used to 'em after a while.'

Patrick nodded, embarrassed at how shaken he was. He realised the deficient lighting was because of a missing bulb from a hanging light fitting, and was relieved he couldn't make out the old woman's features. He wasn't young himself, and didn't want to see the confusion and emptiness that might await him in a decade or two.

He turned away from the old woman and hurried up the stairs.

'Do you want a brew or anything?' the care worker asked in a grudgeful tone.

'No thank you, Marie,' he replied, clocking the name badge

pinned above her ample chest. 'I shouldn't be too long here, but it would be great if you could ensure I'm not disturbed.'

She shrugged. 'I'm not going to stand guard outside if that's what you mean. I wish John had put a bloody lock on the door – it might have saved his life.'

She didn't know he'd been stabbed outside the office before walking back into it to die. More evidence, if any was needed, of her lack of involvement in his death. 'No problem. Anything you can do to leave me in peace while I work will be gratefully appreciated,' he said with his friendliest smile. The coat hanger wire in his pocket seemed to wriggle mischievously in anticipation.

'I'll tell Steph you're here,' she said, as if offering to do him an enormous favour. 'I can't believe they've made her work tonight to be honest – poor thing must still be in shock.' She turned and shuffled off, still muttering to herself.

Patrick left the door open so he could hear if anyone else approached along the corridor; the idea that he might find Mrs Vickers creeping up behind him filled him with irrational terror. Trying to ignore his feelings of unease, he approached the painting and carefully removed it from the wall, ignoring the accusing stare of the long-dead nobleman.

The safe behind it was a simple construct that had been fitted into the wall, similar to the ones commonly found in hotel rooms. There were several ways of cracking this sort of device without knowing the combination. The easiest, unbelievably, was to twist the handle milliseconds after giving the safe a hard strike on the top; this was usually enough to nudge the bolt past the flimsy locking pin inside the door's mechanism. But this would require him to first extract the safe from the brickwork, which would take time and risk leaving unnecessary evidence behind.

Instead, he took out the piece of wire, folding it into a

ninety-degree angle and sliding the end into the small gap between the safe's door and its surround. Then he tilted the makeshift gadget upwards, fiddling around for a button he suspected was located on the door's inside. A few minutes later a satisfying beep told him he'd found the reset switch that enabled the safe's owner to change its locking code. He punched in Andrea's birthday. He knew using his deceased wife's date of birth as his go-to PIN was a maudlin thing to do, but he couldn't help it.

Cancer had taken her from him before he'd left the force, a range of increasingly experimental treatments draining their savings and ultimately doing nothing to prevent the disease's cruel progress. He often wondered what she'd make of his new career. Maybe she was watching him now, laughing at him in her gently mocking way as he skulked in the shadows, spying on people and picking locks like he thought he was some sort of secret agent. He smiled sadly, and re-entered the code. The safe yawned obediently open, its interior momentarily dark and uncertain. Like his future.

Seconds later, Patrick's eyes widened. Not at the sight of the beige folder that he'd seen John Harrington slide into the safe two nights previously, but at the fat bundles of twenty-pound notes stacked on top of it. Momentarily unable to resist, he reached greedily for the money.

Hurried footsteps clicked against the floorboards outside. These were not the comfy flats Marie had been wearing; these shoes were heavy brogues, worn by a man walking quickly and purposefully. Panic exploded in Patrick's chest. There was no time to re-lock the safe, and even if there was, there was certainly no time to hang the portrait back over it. Frantically, he glanced about, leaving the money where it was and the safe hanging open as he dived under the desk.

When the owner of the approaching footwear stepped into

the office, Patrick was concealed from view inches from a twice-cleaned but still clearly visible bloodstain. From his hiding place, he could see that the shoes were smartly polished, attached to elegantly fitted navy-blue trousers. The newcomer paused in the centre of the room, facing the safe. For a few moments the man didn't move at all, and Patrick fought hard to suppress his breathing in the silence. Then a hand reached down to withdraw a mobile phone from one of the trouser pockets.

'Mr Braithwaite, it's Giacomo.' The man's accent matched his name. 'I'm at Brookhaven. The safe is... already open.'

The voice at the other end was an indistinct hiss, but if Patrick strained, he could just about make out what was being said by John Harrington's business partner, whose voice he hadn't heard before.

'What do you mean, "already open"?'

'I don't know, I suppose it must have been the police,' the Italian replied. 'But it's strange: it's still full. I mean, I don't know if they took anything else, but they left... wow.' Giacomo approached the wall with an appreciative whistle. 'There must be about a hundred grand in here, boss!'

Silence from the other end of the line. For someone who'd just learned they had acquired a six-figure cash sum, there was a distinct lack of celebration. Perhaps, to the likes of Harrington and Braithwaite, that amount of money was merely small change. Eventually Patrick heard the muffled crackle of a response.

'Is that all there is?'

'No, there's something else. A folder.' Patrick heard the sound of the interloper rummaging through documents, followed by a delighted exclamation. 'It's the photographs!'

This time Braithwaite emitted an unintelligible bark of satisfaction. Then his tone changed. 'Wait. If the police have been meddling there, we can't touch anything or they'll know. But why the hell would they leave the fucking thing hanging open, with the contents still inside?'

'I... don't know, boss,' Giacomo replied. 'Do you want me to leave it alone?'

'No, you idiot – we can't just leave all that money there unguarded!' Patrick was beginning to feel sorry for Giacomo. There was another pause before Braithwaite continued, a decision reached. 'Leave the money – I can pick it up later. Lock it in the safe with a new code, and don't tell it to anyone but me. But bring the photographs straight here; I might need them tonight.'

'Er, yes, of course, sir. So you... want me to meet you at the Cabin, right now?'

Patrick's interest in the photographs was surpassed only by his intrigue at the mention of 'the Cabin'. Could they be talking about the mysterious place in the woods?

'Yes, right now, and make it quick,' snapped Braithwaite, and he hung up.

'Yes, sir,' said Giacomo disconsolately into the dead line. There was a long pause, before Patrick heard the sound of rummaging in the safe. The man was presumably removing the photographs as instructed.

Then the investigator's heart froze solid, as Giacomo turned and walked straight towards him.

The Italian stopped, close enough for Patrick to see his own reflection in the man's gleaming shoes. The PI held his breath, his entire body as stiff as a coat hanger wire, waiting for Giacomo to stoop and confront him. *Stupid*. He should have tried to brazen it out, masqueraded as a police officer, stuck to his story. Now no silver-tongued explanation would have a chance of holding up. He wondered if Giacomo was the type to call the police, or to drag him out and threaten him with violence. He didn't know which was worse. He hadn't forgotten his police training, and he'd been a talented boxer in his prime; but those days were long gone, and Patrick didn't know how he'd fare against this unknown opponent. He certainly didn't want to have to shoot him.

Then he heard Giacomo whispering numbers in Italian, and realised that he hadn't been spotted at all. Braithwaite's henchman was using the desk to count the money. Long, uncomfortable seconds ticked by, and Patrick thought his lungs might be about to burst. He formed a tiny 'O' with his mouth and tried to silently suck in some much-needed air, but it wasn't enough. He was cramped, dizzy, intolerably tense.

What would Andrea say if she could see him now?

Giacomo seemed to reach a conclusion, muttering what might have been a string of Italian curse words before stuffing some of the money into his own pocket. Patrick almost laughed, wondering how much Giacomo had decided to keep.

Mercifully, Giacomo moved away from the desk, back towards the safe. Patrick heard its door being closed, and five beeps as a new code was entered. He listened as the portrait was hoisted back into position, and relief flooded through him as he watched Giacomo's feet finally pad silently across the beige carpet towards the door.

She'd say you're getting too old for this... but that you should always do the right thing, and always give your best.

He waited until the Italian's shoes had clacked their way back down the corridor, then scrambled out from the indignity of his hiding place, gratefully gulping in lungfuls of air.

She'd say she knows you too well to believe that you'll leave the mystery of the photographs, and this 'Cabin' in the woods, unsolved.

He could easily crack the safe again, take the money for

himself. He could tell Kim Harrington it had been empty, and add her fee to his unexpected windfall.

She'd say you owe it to that poor woman to find out what her husband was doing to get him killed.

'Bloody hell, Andrea,' he muttered to himself as he headed towards the door. His dark sneakers muffled his footsteps as he followed Giacomo along the corridor.

25

MARIE DERBYSHIRE
(CARE WORKER, BROOKHAVEN HALL)

M arie heard Giacomo's footsteps as he descended the stairs. *If that pompous bastard let himself in, he can let himself out*, she thought to herself. Usually, visitors from head office would at least have the courtesy to announce their presence. When she'd heard the door opening and the sound of his fancy shoes clattering their way up the staircase, she'd almost had a coronary. She'd honestly thought it was whoever had killed Mr Harrington, some sharp-suited assassin returned for a second murder spree. The dusting cloth had fallen from her grasp as she'd frozen in place, squatting next to the skirting boards, heart skipping like a broken record player. Then the Italian had rounded the corner, a man she recognised from previous visits accompanying Mr Harrington, and she'd breathed a deep sigh of relief.

'I wasn't snooping!' she blurted, but Giacomo whistled straight past her towards the office, looking stressed-out and miserable.

She really hadn't been snooping. Just keeping an eye on that policeman. There was something shifty about him, and it wasn't because he was black, even though that's what her daughter would accuse her of, because Jade thought everyone who voted for Brexit was a racist. Jade had gotten a lot of funny ideas since she started her A-levels. Too big for her boots, just because she'd gotten good GCSEs and made it into a decent college to study politics. Oh, but she shouldn't criticise her eldest child; she was proud of her daughter, unlike the two boys, who probably wouldn't amount to anything, the troublemaking little sods.

Anyway, here was the black man now, creeping along the corridor moments after Giacomo had left, looking startled to see her crouching there.

'I wasn't snooping!' she reiterated. She *had* overheard the conversation Giacomo had been having, but it wasn't her fault if he'd been speaking too loudly. Strangely, it hadn't been with the policeman at all. Instead, the Italian had been on the phone to someone, someone he called 'sir', which could only mean one person. The other big boss, the one she hadn't met, the one everyone was the most scared of. Some of the stories Greg had told her about Mr Braithwaite...

'That's okay,' replied the policeman, smiling as he recovered his composure. She looked at his scruffy trainers, which she didn't think were what you'd expect a detective to wear. There was definitely something fishy going on. 'You just keep doing what you're doing. You've been very helpful.'

She watched as he hurried off down the corridor. She heard the front door opening, less than a minute after it had closed behind Giacomo. If she strained, she thought she could perhaps hear the sound of a motor starting in the car park, fading as it drove away, echoed by a second vehicle also making its exit.

Ahh well, who cares; better to leave them to it, she thought. Her bones complained loudly as she clambered to her feet. That was another thing Jade didn't understand. *Mum, you should exercise more; Mum, you should eat more healthily, here's some bloody avocado on toast.* Just wait until she got to Marie's age and had three kids, then she'd understand. Marie realised she was muttering some of her thoughts out loud as she plodded towards the office. 'You've been working with nutters too long,' she grumbled, peering into the room. Everything appeared in order. The handsome man in the painting looked down at her, making her think about riches and castles. *Don't forget to put your lottery numbers on for tomorrow.*

She thought about what had happened in that same room, only two nights previously. A businessman stabbed to death, here, in his own office. What was the world coming to, when you weren't even safe in your place of work? She thought about Jade again, a spasm of concern for her daughter assailing her heart, an organ that felt as though it had suffered enough that evening. Better call her, find out how the babysitting was going, whether the boys were behaving themselves or tearing the place apart.

She extracted the archaic phone that Jade had given her when she'd upgraded to a new one, and squinted at the screen. Why did they have to make the bloody things so small? She typed in her daughter's number, which she knew by heart, not like most people nowadays who relied on their phones for everything. Although she did like checking the Facebook; you know, just to see what everybody was up to.

She heard the ringing tone and waited for Jade to answer. Instead, the call went to voicemail.

'It's your mum here. Just making sure you're all okay. I imagine you're watching a film or something,' Marie said, realising she was mainly trying to reassure herself. *More likely the boys are running amok around the estate, torturing the neighbour's cat again.* She tried to dismiss any thoughts of destruction and mischief as she hung up, closing the door behind her as she left the office and its lingering aura of death.

Outside, Steph was waiting in the corridor.

'Bloody hell, is everyone trying to scare me to death tonight?' Marie snapped.

'Sorry,' replied the girl. 'I was coming to ask if you wanted a brew?'

'Aye, go on then.' The older woman realised her colleague looked upset. 'Are you all right, love?' She was a slip of a lass, really. Not even that much older than Jade.

'Yeah, I'm fine.' Steph smiled sadly. 'I just had a bit of a heart to heart with Brian. Telling him all my woes makes me realise how rubbish my life is, I suppose.'

Marie scowled. 'You shouldn't share personal stuff with the residents, you know. Especially not that old crackpot. You know he keeps his granddad's old World War One uniform in his wardrobe?'

Steph laughed. 'I did not know that. He always shows me the rest of his collection, you know, all the old medals and everything.'

'Yeah, none of which are his. He didn't fight in any bloody wars, not like my old dad, God rest his soul. Anyway, I'll come with you to the kitchen.'

They headed towards the stairs. As they approached, a figure appeared at the end of the corridor. Marie's heart felt like it skipped at least three beats.

'Oh, Mrs Vickers, you know you can't come up here!' said Steph, with a lot more patience than Marie could muster. Marie scowled; that bloody copper must have forgotten to close the gate. She watched as Steph led the old woman gently away, thinking once again about her own daughter.

26

JADE DERBYSHIRE

(A-LEVEL STUDENT, AXTON COLLEGE; SUPERMARKET
STOCK ASSISTANT)

'For Christ's sake, Jade, turn that to silent if you aren't going to answer it!'

'Yes, boss,' Jade replied sarcastically, muting the sound of the *Countdown* theme tune. Unlike the others, she didn't feel the need to treat Tammy as if she was some sort of goddess, just because she'd started up their little activists' group. To Jade, she was still Tammy Braithwaite, who Jade had known since school, since long before Ian Braithwaite's daughter had started wearing black eyeliner and fishnets and proclaimed herself a hard-line environmentalist.

Not that she was complaining about Tammy's choice of attire – their self-styled leader looked fantastic. It was no wonder Collin kept staring at her, even though he was ostensibly engaged in a 'thing' with Ayesha, the ditzy girl he'd brought along. Ayesha liked Collin; Collin evidently liked Ayesha; but Jade knew he *really* liked Tammy. If only Tammy was into Ayesha, they'd have quite the love triangle going on. Jade wasn't sure about Lewis, the fledgling group's only other member, but he was gay, so maybe he liked Collin.

And if I wouldn't mind a bit of action with Tammy too, this might even end up as a love pentagram. Not sure if she's into girls though.

Jade slid the phone back into her pocket, knowing her mum would start worrying if she didn't call back soon. But she had no choice but to wait – the old fusspot would only be checking the twins weren't ransacking the place, and Jade had no idea whether they were or not, because she'd left them at home alone, under strict instructions not to screw up while she was out preparing for AEM's grand unveiling.

Her heart wasn't really in all this activism stuff – she was a politics student and thought there were more pressing issues to sort out, not least of which was getting Brexit reversed – but it was nice to be invited, even if she suspected sometimes she was only there because she had a driving licence and a car. But Lewis was funny, and Collin was an old friend, and Tammy was... Tammy. Even the new girl didn't seem too bad in an airheaded sort of way.

And, she had to admit, for someone who felt as world-weary as her name suggested, Jade was finding all this eco-terrorism stuff a lot of fun. The top-secret plan had already been changed once, after Collin's run-in with the policewoman. Tammy's solution was to switch sites, and to get there earlier, so their operation was completed long before any nosy detectives started sniffing around after them.

'Do you really think they even give a shit?' Jade had asked as she'd driven Tammy and Lewis towards the old mine.

'Maybe they think we're something to do with the murder,' said Lewis excitedly, before clapping a hand to his mouth. 'Sorry, Tammy.'

'What are you saying sorry for?' Tammy retorted, raising a dark eyebrow. 'John was my dad's business partner, that's all. They didn't even like each other. At best, he was a sort of weird uncle we hardly ever saw.'

'Anyway, if they *do* think that, they say all publicity is good publicity, am I right?' Jade grinned, putting her foot down as they sped along the empty road.

'All right, but let's not get nicked for speeding before we've even got there,' Lewis stammered, gripping the back seat like a reluctant passenger on a rollercoaster.

'Yeah, and let the police find all the stencils and paint in the back,' Tammy added. 'Slow down a bit, Jade.'

'Yes, boss,' Jade repeated. 'Should I get myself a chauffeur's outfit for next time?'

'It might suit you,' Tammy had replied with a raised eyebrow. *Interesting. Maybe she* was *into girls.* Could be an eventful night ahead, once they'd got the stupid stencil finished and driven back into town.

She watched as Collin and Ayesha hovered, spray cans at the ready.

'Make sure you use consistent, decisive strokes,' coached Lewis, like he was some sort of artistic visionary. The small man, whose dyed black hair matched the colour of his My Chemical Romance T-shirt, was a graphic design student. It had been his idea to use the pre-made stencils after watching a documentary about Banksy. 'They'll be much quicker,' he'd explained when they'd skipped lessons to gather in the pub near college, where they'd planned the mission. 'Plus it can be, you know, our calling card.'

'What, like the Wet Bandits in *Home Alone*?' Jade had been met by three blank stares, and sighed. 'You people are a cultural vacuum, do you know that? This is what I get for taking a year out to earn some money – I'm surrounded by children.'

Now she felt another wisecrack welling up inside her. *Isn't using spray paint to vandalise part of the environment to make a point about preserving the environment kind of... stupid?*

She decided to keep her mouth shut, holding the torch as

steady as she could, illuminating the metal as Lewis's design took shape across it. The AEM logo he'd created, with the letters encircling the globe, looked more like the branding of a right-wing news channel. The slogan beneath, notwithstanding the questionable punctuation she couldn't be bothered to point out, thankfully still made sense despite the change of venue:

STOP DESTROYING
OUR ENVIRONMENT
NO MORE GREEDY DEVELOPERS!

The final *pièce de résistance* was another logo, this time the chunky Harrington and Braithwaite emblem with a huge red cross through it. Tammy might as well have stuck a middle finger right in her father's face. Jade looked at her friend, who was watching excitedly as the paint was applied, and wondered how deep her 'daddy issues' ran.

She'd met Tammy's father before, and found him as creepy as everyone said he was. While Tammy's prominent eyes were cute, his were weird, alien things, jutting so far out of his face they looked as though they might pop out on snail-like stalks. She'd eaten silently at the family's kitchen table while those unblinking orbs had ogled her, and Tammy's mum had slurred her way through some drunken anecdote.

Jade shivered, and not just because of the chill air. Its frostbitten edge helped bring her back to the present moment, and she glanced around at their surroundings as she took a sip from the plastic bottle of energy drink she'd brought with her. They'd chosen the entrance to the old mine, or more accurately the intimidating and rusted metal slab that sealed off the tunnel, as the canvas for Lewis's graffiti. It was at the end of a cleft that had been hewn into the hillside, which loomed above them like a giant boulder before sloping away into the picturesque countryside that undulated down towards the river.

Climbing the sheer rock face was impossible, so the only exits from this place were either back towards the road about a quarter of a mile behind them, where they'd hidden their cars amongst the nearby trees, or by traversing the forest itself, whose dark expanse stretched away on their right-hand side. To the left, a rockfall or shaft collapse had created a gaping pit, which was surrounded by flimsy-looking high-vis safety barriers. Some of these were missing – stolen or perhaps blown into the abyss – making the area dangerous to approach. The AEM's entire army was, in effect, trapped at the end of a long cul-de-sac, half natural and half man-made.

Jade looked at the hunk of metal that had been used to close off the mine entrance, thinking about how perilous an existence it must have been to work beyond it. Filthy, choking on stale air and potentially poisonous fumes, worrying the tunnel might crumble onto your skull at any moment. The problems poor people had grappled with decades ago were very different from fretting about losing a few TikTok followers.

'Will anyone even see this?' Ayesha asked. Tammy had answered by projecting daggers through several layers of eyeshadow.

'Course they will,' said Collin. 'But let's hurry up, so we can get into town and get drinking... why don't you take over for a bit, Jade?'

But Jade wasn't paying attention to him. Instead, her gaze had drifted back towards the road, where a sudden glare of illumination had caught her attention.

'Is that a car?' she said, puzzled.

'It's a road, so probably,' quipped Collin.

'Is it coming this way?' asked Tammy worriedly, frowning as she squinted in the same direction.

'No,' said Jade, frowning at the pair of lights. 'It's just... waiting there.'

Collin and Ayesha stopped what they were doing, and the five of them turned towards the glow. If Jade listened carefully, she thought she could hear the vehicle's engine ticking over.

'Who the hell is that?' whispered Lewis. 'Do you think they've seen us?'

'Is it the police?' asked Ayesha, her voice trembling.

'Just ignore them,' said Tammy. 'Get this finished and then we'll march straight out of here. They'll think we were having a party or whatever. No big deal.'

Jade continued to stare at the headlights. Surrounded by blackness, they seemed to stare back.

27

BRUNO BERZINS

(CONSTRUCTION OPERATIVE AND 'ODD JOB MAN', HARRINGTON AND BRAITHWAITE PROPERTY GROUP)

B runo was also staring at the lights. Completely oblivious to the presence of Jade and the others, who were about five hundred yards to his rear, he was watching the car from inside the forest. It was his own vehicle, and he'd left it idling about a quarter of a mile away from where he was now hunkered down. He was quite comfortable in the dirt, the smoke from his carefully rolled joint and the occasional motion of his hand towards his lips as he inhaled its marijuana fumes the only movements that might betray his presence. Only someone with superhuman eyesight, or wearing night vision goggles, would spot them. Bruno was as invisible as all the other creatures that crawled, and scuttled, and skulked amongst the trees.

Unlike the five members of the AEM, Bruno was not using his naked eyes to observe the vehicle. Instead, he was watching it through the scope of his sniper rifle, the Dragunov SVD he'd managed to take with him when he left the Latvian military, thanks to his contact in the army's Logistics division. The gun had made the journey with him to the UK when he moved there in the year 2000, shortly before 9/11 had ushered in a new millennium of fear and paranoia, along with tighter airport security. That was when Ian Braithwaite had first offered him a job, albeit one without a title. 'Fixer' might be appropriate. 'Odd job man', as he sometimes called himself.

To be honest, he'd been delighted when Braithwaite had called him late the previous night. It was nice to feel useful again, to feel he could offer something other than hard and menial labour on the construction site. He knew there was other demand for his skills, but that would mean engaging with a criminal underworld he didn't know well, in a language that he still found difficult after so many years. Stupid words and phrases like 'eventually' or 'sooner or later' or 'after all', which seemed to mean the same as each other, but didn't at all. Ah well. Eventually, sooner or later, after all, he knew that his target would arrive.

And that he would die.

He hadn't smoked pot back when he was in the army, but if anything, he'd found that its relaxing effects made his shooting even more accurate. Plus, since he used to smoke forty cigarettes a day back in those days, graduating onto weed was probably healthier too. Probably. Some people said it messed up your brain. His felt pretty messed up already. Your dad being killed in front of you had that effect.

Anyway, he mustn't let his thoughts wander. He had a job to do. A job with simple instructions, issued in a familiar hoarse and worried-sounding rasp. In fact, Braithwaite had sounded more than worried. What was the word? *Desperate.*

That prick Potter won't come himself. He'll send someone else, whoever he hired to murder John. They'll have instructions to kill me too. You need to get the jump on them, then get rid of their body and the car.

Another strange phrase. 'Get the jump on them'. He understood that it wasn't meant literally. He wouldn't be jumping on anyone. In fact, he'd barely be moving at all.

Nothing more than a gentle squeeze of the trigger, a single round speeding towards his target's skull at close to 1,000 feet per second. If his ploy worked, they'd wander over to investigate the abandoned car, perhaps thinking that Braithwaite was waiting inside it for them to approach him. They'd probably bring their own weapon, concealed in a jacket pocket, ready to blast him through the driver's side window. Bruno would wait for them to pause, frowning at the empty seat. Then it would be their brains getting splattered all over the glass.

He wasn't looking forward to cleaning them off.

Still, if that was all he had to worry about, the job would have gone well. *Swimmingly*, as people said. It would be trickier if more than one assassin showed up. Bruno had already asked Braithwaite what to do in that eventuality. His boss had been unequivocal.

'Kill them all. I doubt Potter has the money or the clout to rustle up a whole squad, but if he does, it's better if none of them are still around to come after me for revenge.'

He took another drag on the joint, allowing his eyes to close briefly, savouring the smoke as it rolled down his throat and into his expectant lungs.

There'd been smoke that day too; the day that had become known as the Day of the Barricades. As the new Latvian government had feared, the USSR had tried to retake the country soon after its declaration of independence in 1990. The OMON had already launched an attack on Lithuania, and officials believed Riga was next. They were right. The city's preparations had ensured the Russians were repelled with minimal casualties. Not just by the Latvian military, but by ordinary people like his father, people armed with pieces of metal and Molotov cocktails, forming human shields around potential strategic targets.

The departing Soviets had put a bullet in the old man's head as a parting shot. A final *fuck you* from a crumbling empire. Bruno, a devastated teenager, had known even then that he would become a soldier. Like the famous Latvian Riflemen his father had told him stories about, he would defend his family with his wits and his trusty firearm.

Now look at you, Bruno. Defending nothing but an old crook.

He smiled mirthlessly, flicking the remnants of the spliff into some nearby leaves. His homeland and his conscience had lost any sway they had over him years ago. Just like the world around him, Bruno had moved on.

Lights carved the darkness, appearing in the distance and approaching his car from the direction he'd left it facing, away from his temporary sniper's nest. It might only be another evening motorist, speeding past on their way to the outskirts of town, perhaps even a rare visitor from outside making a hasty exit. But Bruno had a feeling the car would slow down when it saw the headlights, perhaps stopping a hundred metres away, maybe drawing nose to nose with his vehicle. It depended how ballsy the driver was. Maybe they would lean out of the driver's window and shoot at the car, smelling a rat immediately. Either way, their skull would soon be just like his dad's, split apart like a coconut, seeping its juices into the dirt. A worthless and broken vessel, that couldn't be repaired.

At fifty feet away, the car stopped. A black 4x4, with a front bumper that had seen better days. Close enough for him to make out the shapes of at least two men, one in each of the front seats. Hopefully they'd both get out, and he could pick them off in quick succession, before the second even had a chance to react to his friend's brain vaporising right in front of him.

But they didn't. Instead they remained sitting there, dark shapes moving towards each other, like merging shadows. They were talking. Maybe they were close enough to see that the car was unoccupied in the glare of their headlights. Maybe they'd drive away. He might be able to pick the driver off from here, through the windscreen. But for all he knew there were three more guys in the back seat, armed with rifles of their own, or baseball bats and hammers. No need to take any chances, not yet.

It started to rain as the passenger door opened. An enormous man unfolded himself from the seat, bald and broad-shouldered, reminding Bruno of the killer from a slasher movie. But this man didn't shamble slowly towards him like the plodding maniacs in those stupid films. Instead, he strode purposefully through the sudden downpour, not even bothering to conceal the pistol Bruno recognised immediately as a Glock 17, as ubiquitous as guns could get. It meant this guy could be anything from a drug dealer to an undercover cop.

The big man stooped forwards as he marched towards Bruno's car, head tucked into his chest as though he anticipated a trap. His movements were precise and methodical, aiming his weapon at the windscreen as he approached. Ex-military, maybe, just like Bruno. *This could be trickier than I thought.*

The next few moments seemed impossibly slow, each microsecond expanded into oceans of time. Bruno sensed every heartbeat, heard every raindrop. He felt the years between two gunshots compressed into a single moment. A Russian soldier squeezing a trigger in 1991; a washed-up old Latvian construction worker repeating the feat almost thirty years later.

Maybe it was just the weed.

Lightning flared in the sky, illuminating the bald man's face clearly, as well as the inside of Bruno's empty vehicle. The giant was freeze-framed, aghast, for a single instant. At the same time, the driver of his own car leaned out of his window, a fat man whose neck flesh wobbled like a turkey's as he called to his companion. 'What's up?'

The bald man whirled, shouting back, already starting to propel himself into a run. 'It's a–'

Bruno's bullet entered the back of his skull, then blasted out through his forehead in a spray of bloody gristle. Calmly, Bruno shifted the barrel towards the second man, who appeared too shocked even to retract his head, and fired again. The round went through the fat man's brain, through the rear driver's side window, back into the car and out through the back window once again, flesh and bone and glass altering its trajectory only imperceptibly. The two bullets would come to rest somewhere in the woods. Perhaps squirrels would helpfully bury them, thinking they were shiny acorns. It didn't matter. No one would ever find his rifle, which he kept hidden in a secret compartment behind his refrigerator.

Bruno waited, stock-still. He was already drenched by the unanticipated deluge, but didn't yet know if there was anyone else in the car, anyone he might see diving into the front of the vehicle to take the wheel and reverse out of the kill zone.

The car didn't move. Nothing moved. The only sound was the thunder, and the rain, which bucketed down as if it was trying to cleanse the earth of the mess Bruno had made.

He clambered to his feet without allowing his body's groan of discontent to emerge from his lips. *Complaining was for idiots like Daniel Glebe, that fucking moron who couldn't even learn to drive, who gambled away his wife's money and then complained she worked too much.* Trudging across to his fallen marks, he did permit himself a low whistle at the sheer size of the crumpled giant. He looked more like a shaved silverback than a man. *All those hours in the gym didn't make you tough enough to repel a bullet, did they, Mr Big Stuff?* In Bruno's experience, men like that were vain and unpleasant. Strong of body, weak of mind. He was sure this one was no exception.

Allowing himself a smile of satisfaction, he moved towards

his own car, opening the door to switch the headlights and the engine off. No point wasting fuel now that the job was done. He sidled across to the second vehicle, intending to do the same once he'd inspected the other body. It had slumped face first through the open window, the back of its head displaying the gruesome exit wound like a bizarre new haircut. Bruno opened the door and the corpse spilled out like – what was the phrase? *A sack of shit.* He enjoyed that one. It landed face-up in the muck at his feet, eyes wide and perplexed.

Oh fuck.

Another moment, another freeze-frame.

No way.

A face he recognised instantly as the lightning flared, illuminating it in a spectral shade of blue.

It can't be.

The face staring up at him from the sludge belonged to the politician, Eric Potter. The man Ian Braithwaite had been adamant wouldn't attend in person.

A man whose death wasn't so easy to sweep under the carpet.

Both bodies were far too heavy for him to carry, for different reasons. Hoisting them under the armpits and dragging them down the trail was an option, albeit an unappealing one: it would take forever, and leave him exhausted. Instead, he managed to heave them into the 4x4, grimacing at the unspeakable fluids their shattered skulls seeped onto his clothes, glad of the rain to at least partially wash them off. Not that it mattered; his wife wouldn't ask any questions. Monica was used to him arriving home covered in blood. She was a good woman, and she knew how he earned his extra money.

He manhandled Potter's carcass into the back seat where it sprawled, warm and stinking, like a harpooned whale. As often happened, the contents of the politician's bowels had evacuated shortly after his heart had stopped beating. Bruno ruminated on the indignity of death, as well as on what Potter might have had as his last meal. Unlike men on death row, most people aren't afforded the luxury of choosing something suitably momentous.

The bald man went into the boot. Bruno grunted as he lifted the heavyweight onto the conveniently-positioned load lip, depositing him there while he recovered his breath. The dead man reminded him of a hiker, sitting down after a strenuous excursion into the woods, his chin sagging forwards to rest against his broad chest as though he was nodding off. The rain filled the open ruin of his skull like beer poured into an overflowing jug.

Bruno pushed him backwards into the generous cargo space, and slammed the door.

He hadn't driven a car that size for years, and it took him a while to figure out how to get it into gear. His own vehicle was an ancient sedan, with only five gears to choose from. This was some modern monstrosity with special off-road settings, or whatever the hell they were. He felt again the increasingly familiar sense of the world slowly moving forwards around him, trying to leave him behind.

Yet Bruno persisted. *Plenty of gas in the tank. Just like this crackpot car.* That diesel fuel would be useful soon, when he needed to burn the stupid contraption up.

He drove the car towards the old mine entrance, tree branches scraping and knocking against its exterior like angry demonstrators appalled at his crime. He stopped close to the sealed-off opening, illuminating the metal barricade with his headlights. It had been daubed with some mural, recently painted. Clearly his employer was as unpopular with the ecoterrorists as he was with his own workforce. He smirked at it, then turned his attention to the bright orange barriers that delineated the outline of the nearby pit.

It was a pity the collapsed shaft wasn't wide and deep enough for him to dump the car itself down there, but the chasm would certainly swallow up two corpses, no matter how muscular – or fat and foul smelling – they were. He dragged the huge man to the precipice first, letting gravity carry the giant down into the void when Bruno released his grip. The bald man tumbled like some stupid drunk that had wandered into a ravine.

Potter went next, sliding downwards more slowly, as if he was too big for the pit to swallow in one go. Bruno chewed his lip anxiously as he watched the reeking cadaver slide out of view. Hired mercenaries didn't usually leave behind much in the way of grieving friends and family, but a high-profile fucking politician; that was someone who would be missed, would be searched for. If the 4x4 belonged to Potter, and Bruno left it here as a burnt-out wreck, he might as well also leave a glaring neon sign saying *this way for the dead MP*. Bruno was wearing latex gloves, and his DNA wasn't on any UK police database, but there was no guarantee he hadn't left behind something incriminating, some microscopic shred that would lead the police to his door.

Better if the bodies were never found.

He turned back towards the car, and took out his mobile phone. Braithwaite answered after the second ring.

'Is it done?'

'Yeah. Just one guy,' he lied. 'His body's in the pit, but I will take his car out of town before I burn it. You can send me the money now.' There was no need to tell him about the politician. Once his disappearance was all over the news, Braithwaite could suspect whatever he wanted to. Bruno would have his pay cheque by then.

'Good. I knew I could count on you.' Braithwaite hung up. Bruno smiled, and opened the car door.

Then he froze, brain skewered by shock and confusion.

Somewhere to his left, near the rusted chunk of metal that covered the mine entrance, he could hear music playing.

Music he recognised, from one of the TV shows that his wife liked.

28

LEWIS JONES

(A-LEVEL STUDENT, AXTON COLLEGE; GLASS
COLLECTOR, SWAN AND RAILWAY PUB)

'He heard your phone, Jade! *Run!*'

There had been a split second, a fleeting moment after his friend's ringtone had sounded, when Lewis had truly believed he was inside a bad dream. Perhaps it was the overwhelming surreality of the situation: the five of them, cowering behind a half-rotted steel slab inside a century-old mineshaft that might collapse on their heads at any moment, being soundtracked by the *Countdown* clock. The otherworldly presence of the short, burly man that had thrown two human corpses into an open hole in the ground in the manner of someone disposing of two bin bags, then chatted nonchalantly to someone on his phone. The same man, now turning to stare at them, eyes wide with shock and violence; that was the moment when Lewis was certain he would wake up.

He didn't. Instead, the man started sprinting towards them, and they all screamed and fled into the tunnel.

Even when they'd heard the two gunshots earlier, Lewis hadn't truly believed they were in danger. It could have been fireworks, or a backfiring car engine. But they'd been frightened enough to decide to hide, and to switch off their torches. Now

Jade had fumbled hers back on, illuminating the oppressive cavern that narrowed ahead of them. He felt like a morsel of food disappearing into an intestine.

'Turn that off, or he'll know where we are!' Tammy hissed.

'But how will we bloody see where we're going?' Jade snapped back.

'We just need to stay away from him until the police arrive,' said Collin, his usual bluster diminished to a frightened whisper. Lewis hoped he was right. When the first corpse had tumbled into the ravine, Jade had risked calling the authorities, frantically whispering the specifics of their situation. For all Lewis knew, it was the police returning her call that had landed them in this mess.

He prayed they'd been taken seriously, and that a carload of officers were on their way.

'What if it's a dead end?' whimpered Ayesha, sounding terrified.

'Then we'll have to fight him,' said Jade grimly. 'There are five of us and only one of him.'

'He's got a fucking *gun*, Jade,' snarled Tammy. 'You can't fight bullets! And did you see the size of that bloke he threw into the pit? If he can kill *him*, he won't have any problem killing us, will he?'

Lewis stayed quiet, wishing he exercised more, concentrating on his breathing while he tried to sustain their punishing pace, and on trying not to stumble on the increasingly rough-hewn rock floor. The tunnel was leading them downwards in a shallow incline, and he felt panic swelling within him, a sense that they were leaving civilisation and rationality behind the deeper they went.

'We should split up,' said Tammy. 'That way some of us have more chance of getting back out to get help.'

'Are you bloody joking?' barked Jade. 'We're sticking together! You know, how friends do?'

The temperature seemed to be rising as they staggered onwards. He thought of the hellish scenes he'd glimpsed in movies, of long-buried evils and brimstone, of balrogs and lava pits and inescapable death. He knew the heat was probably due to their frenzied pace, but this was no comfort, because he realised he couldn't maintain that speed for much longer. It would be him: the first one to fall, the one their stalker would trip over in the darkness, the one who'd be dragged to his feet and beaten to death, or shot, or both.

Oh God, this couldn't be happening. This couldn't be real. *Please let me wake up, sweating and shivering in my bed, worrying about normal things like exam results, or my parents finding out I smoke, or–*

An arm encircled his shoulders and a hand clamped over his mouth, and he was yanked suddenly to his left. His horrified scream was muffled by the fingers pressed tightly over his lips, and his friends heard nothing; they just kept running, their frightened chatter and Jade's torchlight disappearing quickly into the blackness.

'*Shhh,*' breathed a voice close to his ear. 'It's me.' A face was illuminated briefly by the light from a phone screen, before it was hastily clicked off. It was Tammy. She'd hauled him into some sort of cramped side passage. 'Don't start fucking screaming, okay?' She removed her hand slowly from his face. The darkness was absolute.

'What are you doing?' he whispered, almost hyperventilating. 'What about the others?'

'Like I said, we need to split up. When he runs past, you and I can–'

She was interrupted by the sound of footsteps, and fastened her hand across his mouth once again. Lewis didn't mind; a scream was welling up inside his chest, and he needed all the help he could get not to let it burst out of him. What they were doing felt like a betrayal, but he was too terrified to care. In the main tunnel to their right, the footfalls approached, the scrape of shoes on stone. A torch beam danced into view, like the light from some subterranean fairy, fleeing in terror from the same murderous pursuer.

The footsteps slowed, their sound accompanied by deep, panting breaths. Then a voice, accented, Eastern European. 'Come on now,' it wheezed. 'There is no need to run. We can figure it out.'

Lewis felt Tammy shaking next to him, and realised he was trembling too. The clatter of his teeth rattling against each other sounded deafening. His heart pounded, his blood roared. It was impossible that this man wouldn't hear the noises their quaking bodies were making. They would die down here, in an abandoned mine, their bodies tossed into an open pit like old furniture into a landfill site.

Then the man growled something in what might have been Russian, and his footsteps continued along the tunnel, moving past them.

'Go on,' whispered Tammy, nudging Lewis in the ribs. 'Just go, *now*.' But he couldn't. He was paralysed, as if the coarse stone of the walls and floor had grown around him, encasing his hands and feet. 'Lewis!' his friend hissed. She might as well have been berating a statue. 'Fine, suit yourself,' Tammy said in exasperation, squeezing past him in the darkness. 'I don't know why I even tried to help y–'

Her rebuke was cut off by her own cry as she tripped and fell. Lewis heard a nasty smack as she hit the floor, a too-loud moan of pain.

The next sound he heard was another gunshot, followed by a noise like a projectile colliding with a wet pillow. When he heard Tammy's voice again, her groans had been reshaped into screams.

Lewis ran. He clambered over his wounded friend, and he ran. He ran from her howls of pain, and from the footsteps as the shooter scrambled back up the tunnel. He ran from the man's unintelligible threats. He ran from the torchlight that reached for him, falling short, and from the gunshot that blasted a bullet in his direction, grazing his ear on its way past.

He ran towards the sliver of light through which they'd squeezed, five of them, reduced now to four.

29

ZACHARIASZ WOZNIAK

(CONSTABLE, CHESHIRE CONSTABULARY)

*Z*ack heard the gunshots as he clambered out of the patrol car. He'd been sceptical about the story he'd heard on dispatch, about some teens who thought they'd seen a body being dumped into the collapsed mineshaft. It sounded like the plot of a Tarantino movie. But the cars he'd seen had certainly been suspicious: two hidden in the trees along the main road, another by the roadside, and now a 4x4 parked suspiciously close to the exposed pit, its front bumper badly damaged. All the vehicles were empty.

But Zack was no longer thinking about the cars. Instead, he had radioed the station and was hurrying towards the mine entrance, from where the gunshots had emanated. As he approached the thick metal seal, which had been painted over by some fresh-looking graffiti, he could see it had been prised loose, leaving a gap through which someone might squeeze into the tunnels beyond.

Could be a stupid wind-up, he thought. *Youngsters mucking about.* But the blasts hadn't sounded like a BB gun or a firework going off. And even if it was only some silly kids letting off pyrotechnics in there, they were liable to bring the whole hillside tumbling down on top of them.

Suddenly a man burst out from behind the barrier, gasping as he tore his clothes and skin on the metal. Zack intercepted him, pressing a sturdy forearm across the man's torso and pinning him against the rock wall.

'What's going on in there?' he asked firmly.

The man, who he could now see was little more than a teenager, wriggled ineffectually in his grasp. 'He's coming,' the youngster panted. 'He's got a gun!'

Zack wasn't too much older than the boy himself, and had been in the job for only a couple of years. Although the level of crime in and around Axton was usually limited to drunken violence at weekends, he had already faced a number of complex confrontations. The split-second decision-making that was required was a test of his training, and of his nerve. Yes, this kid might be telling the truth. But he also might be carrying a weapon of his own, and if Zack wasn't careful, he could end up stabbed.

He turned the boy around and held him against the wall. 'Hands up,' he barked. He had no grounds to make an arrest, which meant the youth technically had no reason to comply. Nevertheless, the lad didn't struggle, suddenly limp with fear as Zack patted him down. Wallet, phone, keys. Nothing untoward.

'He shot her,' the boy whimpered.

'Okay,' the policeman said, turning the youth around to face him once again. 'Just tell me what's happened.'

Then he felt something cold pressed against the side of his head. The boy emitted a little sob of terror.

'Don't move, and don't look at me,' said a voice from the darkness beyond the mine entrance. From the corner of his eye, Zack could see a long rifle barrel jutting out of the gloom. 'The only way you live is if you don't see my face. Understand?'

The weapon's owner was no teenager. His voice was gruff and cold, with an Eastern European accent. Not Polish, like Zack's father, but not dissimilar. The constable nodded slowly, keeping his eyes trained on the kid in front of him. He twitched his head sideways, trying to encourage the boy to flee into the forest, but the lad seemed frozen in shock.

'This is a Dragunov sniper rifle,' continued the voice. 'Old but reliable. Like me. With it I am a, what do you call it, a crack shot. I'm going to come out, and you're both going to stay very still, like statues, while I walk to my car. I will be walking backwards, pointing this gun at you. So if you move before you hear me drive away, your head will go pop like JFK.'

'What... what about me?' the boy snivelled. 'I didn't see your face either, I promise.'

'That's good for you,' replied the shooter. 'Now turn around and face the wall.'

He's going to kill both of us, Zack thought. *He has no reason not to.* If he really was armed with a sniper rifle, he'd probably wait until he was far enough away before picking them off. Or he could just execute them right now, at point blank range through the crack in the door. Which meant this was Zack's best and only chance to do something. But with the gun jammed into his temple, his options were extremely limited.

He heard the shooter grunting as he squeezed out through the aperture, clearly not sharing the teenager's slight build. But the man didn't loosen his grip on his weapon, didn't allow the barrel to waver from its position for even a split second. *Grab it,* Zack mimed to the boy, gesturing with his eyes once again. But the kid seemed to have lapsed into a catatonic trance, no longer even meeting Zack's gaze. To his right, Zack discerned the shape of his enemy, a thickset man wearing dark clothing, sidestepping carefully towards his rear. A tight crop of greying hair. Old, experienced. Calm.

'My colleagues are on their way here,' Zack said carefully. 'You won't get far. It's better if you just stop this, and hand over the weapon.'

The gun pressed harder into his skull, forcing his head into an awkward sideways angle. 'It's better if you shut your mouth, unless you and the boy want to die.'

'What's happened in there?' Zack persisted. 'Does someone need medical attention?'

'Yes!' cried the boy, the memory of his recent trauma seeming to snap him back to life. 'He shot Tammy!'

The mention of that name was as though a magic spell had been cast. The rifleman's composure evaporated, and he shifted his weapon towards the boy, ramming the barrel into the centre of his forehead.

'What did you say?' the gunman shouted. 'Did you say... *Tammy?*' The man's voice faltered, full of disbelief. Maybe even horror.

Zack knew he wouldn't get a better opportunity. He thrust his hands upwards, jerking the gun towards the sky before heaving it down, twisting as he did so, using his bodyweight to prise the weapon out of the man's grip. It clattered to the floor as the man barrelled into him, ploughing Zack into the jagged stone of the wall.

'Get the gun!' Zack shouted, and the boy reacted, kicking the weapon away from the shooter as the man stooped to collect it. The youth evaded the man's flailing grasp and stumbled forwards, falling across the weapon. Now the gunman was caught between two options: the boy, sprawled on top of his rifle on the ground, and the policeman behind him, not yet subdued.

The shooter deemed Zack to be the bigger threat. The young officer was a capable fighter, but had no answer to the lunging headbutt that was deployed against him, his assailant as aggressive as a rutting goat. The vicious blow connected with his upper chest, and Zack felt his ribs buckle as the wind gusted out of him. He sagged down onto the wet ground with his back against the wall. The man, who was dressed in a nondescript tracksuit and smelled of marijuana, hovered over him, something desperate and dangerous twisting in his eyes. Zack tried to clamber to his feet, but it was useless. He could barely even catch his breath. Satisfied that Zack was incapacitated, the man turned towards the boy. Then he froze.

The boy was pointing the rifle at him.

Each silent second was like an explosion of pain in Zack's ribcage. He wondered if he was bleeding internally, if a shard of bone was jutting into his windpipe. What an unfortunate ending to his short career, if he was to drown in his own blood, slain by a single blow. He thought about his wife. His vision blurred for a moment, a few seconds lost. When his consciousness returned, the man had advanced a few steps towards the boy, who was crawling backwards on his buttocks, trembling as he aimed the gun.

'Tell me again,' the man said. His voice sounded cold, but fragile. Teetering on the brink of some huge collapse. 'The girl with you. Her name.'

'Her name is Tammy,' the boy replied. His words dripped with vengeful fury. 'And she might still survive, if you'd let us get help for her.'

'She is... the daughter of Ian Braithwaite?' The man's voice was as cold as a Baltic wind.

The boy nodded. A strange shudder passed through the man, and he sank to his knees. Zack stared, uncomprehending, every inhalation searing his chest. In the distance, he thought he could hear a car approaching.

Everything moved in slow motion, as though beheld through gallons of liquid. The man reached towards his pocket. Zack lurched forwards, trying desperately to propel himself towards him. The floor rushed upwards to meet him as he collapsed face first in the muck, groaning with agony.

As a pair of headlights appeared at the end of the trail, the man removed a mobile phone. Still the boy jabbed the rifle towards his tormentor, shaking and sobbing. Zack strained to listen as the sound of his bloodstream swirled in his ears, and the headlights bounced towards them.

The man's call was answered after several rings.

'I am sorry, Yuri,' the gunman said to whoever had picked up. 'There has been... a big mistake.'

The car swerved to a stop nearby, and a police officer leapt out of it. Through the haze of his vision, Zack recognised his colleague, DI Friedel, shouting as he sprinted towards them.

The man reached towards his other pocket, withdrawing a small pistol. Friedel dived towards him as he tucked it under his own chin.

Zack was unsure whether he heard, or imagined, the sound of the gunshot as he slipped into unconsciousness.

30

VINCE REYNOLDS

(FREELANCE SECURITY GUARD)

Vince chewed his chewing gum, and thought about death. It was on his mind a lot. He'd been around it all his life, to the point where he thought perhaps his very presence was its harbinger. His mother had died in childbirth, his alcoholic dad of liver failure a few years later. His first foster father had died in a car crash. His second had mysteriously fallen down the stairs and broken his neck. The last one was when Vince had learned that death wasn't always something that happened to others at random. It was a force you could control, and even command.

But mortality hadn't lost its power to shock him. John Harrington's demise had come out of the blue, and Vince still didn't know what it meant for him. He worked for Harrington and Braithwaite, but he'd always considered himself John's employee. The businessman had approached him after witnessing him strongarm three troublemakers out of the nightclub he used to work in, leaving only one of them able to walk. 'You're the sort of man we need for a new business venture,' the tycoon had said later, handing him a business card.

'Give me a call tomorrow if you're interested in some better-paid work.'

That had been three years ago, and that phone call had led him here, to the Cabin, where he was now the head of security. He'd seen a lot of things in his time here; local celebrities, criminals, politicians and other powerful people. The girls they preferred to spend time with, all of them different. Blondes, brunettes, redheads. Black girls, white girls, girls from South America or Bulgaria or Peckham. Girls who liked chatting to him and squeezing his thick biceps. Girls who were terrified of him. Girls who were long-term regulars, who'd been coming here since before him.

Girls who angered John Harrington.

Girls who didn't last long.

Girls he'd had to help make disappear.

For an old timer, his boss's appetites had been voracious. He was at the Cabin at least once a week, especially when there was a new lass. He offered them to Vince sometimes, calling it 'a perk of the job'. Vince usually accepted. After all, he didn't have a missus of his own. Women were too unpredictable, too confusing. They seemed to be drawn to his violence, but always fled from it, acting so surprised the first time he hit them. What did they expect from a man like him? The point was, he felt he understood John Harrington. Like Vince, Harrington was a man, with a man's needs and a man's impulses. A man's temper.

Braithwaite, on the other hand, never slept with the girls. There was something deeply chilling about him. He reminded Vince of a ghost, wafting silently around the premises as though his feet were hovering centimetres above the floor, mimicking the appearance of footsteps. He often turned up unannounced, his black Chrysler rolling slowly up the dirt track like a funeral hearse. Vince honestly wouldn't have been surprised if

Braithwaite emerged not from the driver's seat, but from a coffin in the back.

And now Harrington was dead, leaving the weirdo as his only remaining boss. Vince was convinced Braithwaite was responsible for the slaying. And that meant Braithwaite had someone else, some killer other than Vince, to turn to for his dirty work. Which meant Vince was vulnerable.

Vince didn't like feeling vulnerable.

He tried to forget about it, concentrating on the job in hand. He was standing guard outside the main door, a task he would normally delegate to one of his small team of like-minded contractors, but not on a night of such importance. The Cabin's front entrance had a wooden porch, which had protected him from the sudden downpour, but not from the bitter November wind that sliced through his dark overcoat like a switchblade. He didn't mind. It helped him focus, as did the chewing gum. His eyes were trained on the dirt trail, watching for any sign that their VIP guest was arriving.

He glanced around at the dark outlines of the trees, at the twisted shapes of the trunks and branches, putting him in mind of an angry mob of malformed people slowly advancing upon him. The trees had nothing to be angry about. The woods were complicit, as guilty as he was. He killed the girls, and the forest swallowed them up like pagan offerings. Like compost.

No one ever came looking for them.

Minutes passed, and nobody appeared on the trail. Nigel Hawke, the Tory MP candidate, was late. Vince didn't like Tories. This one was probably as much of an arrogant cunt as the rest of them. It wasn't political; he just didn't like posh boys. Public school toffs who'd probably never worked a proper day in their lives, never been in a fight. Never had to shove their pervert stepdad down the stairs.

He remembered the last politician that had visited the Cabin. The Labour MP, Eric Potter. Harrington had told Vince he'd pay him extra if he peeked in through the window and grabbed a few choice shots on his camera phone. Vince had been happy to oblige. He often took a peep at what the girls were up to anyway. A perk of the job.

There was a flash of something amongst the trees, maybe light glinting off a metallic surface. Vince squinted towards it, frowning, pausing his chewing motion for a moment. Whatever it was did not reappear. The front door opened behind him, and he turned to see Ian Braithwaite looming there like a vampire. His employer looked uncharacteristically rattled, lowering his mobile phone from his ear.

'Any sign of Hawke yet?' Braithwaite snapped irritably. His skin looked even paler than usual, as if it had started to prematurely rot. Vince shook his head. 'I... might need to go somewhere, unexpectedly,' the old man continued. 'Giacomo will manage Hawke if he arrives before I get back.' His boss's secretary – or whatever jumped-up title he used – had arrived half an hour previously, looking as slick and slimy as always, like a half-amphibian creature.

'Okay, boss,' Vince said taciturnly, turning the gum over in his mouth.

'Just make sure nothing goes wrong,' Braithwaite said, jabbing a finger towards him. It looked as thin and bony as an old twig. 'We can't afford to fuck this up, okay?'

With that, the old man strode past Vince and out into the freezing air. The security guard watched him cross to his Chrysler, glancing again towards the forest, trying to pinpoint the flicker of light he'd seen earlier. Nothing. The wind swirled, and Vince chewed, and the trees whispered like conspirators. Above him, the swollen rain clouds contemplated another assault.

Then Vince heard the sound of another car approaching. Braithwaite heard it too, the old man swearing and muttering under his breath as he abandoned his car, turning to hurry back towards the Cabin. Vince watched as a BMW crunched its way up the pathway towards them.

31

NIGEL HAWKE

(POLITICIAN, CONSERVATIVE PARTY CANDIDATE FOR AXTON AND MIDDLEWICH)

'I'm sorry, but I've been called away on an urgent family matter,' said Braithwaite, who was as foul as Nigel remembered from their last meeting. The older man's voice and the smell of his breath made him think of fetid air released from some unearthed sarcophagus. 'I'll be leaving you in the capable hands of Giacomo here for an hour or so.'

Nigel, whose friends all called him Nige, returned his host's disingenuous smile. Braithwaite's Italian lackey hovered behind, wearing a smile even less sincere than his boss's. The expression looked like he stored it overnight in a jar of preserving chemicals.

'Don't worry,' Nige replied. 'I wasn't expecting to be talking business, if you know what I mean.'

He winked, and Giacomo laughed as if he'd cracked the most hilarious joke of the new millennium. Braithwaite's forced chuckle made Nige's blood squirm.

'Why don't you follow me, sir?' Giacomo asked, and Nige allowed the stooge to escort him towards the door, past the gormless brute they had manning it. Nige wondered, as he often did when faced with the sorts of thuggish chavs that would soon be his constituents, what life must be like when you were all muscle and no brain. He imagined it was quite liberating, akin to the existence of a faithful dog: going through the motions of life, unencumbered by ambition or self-awareness. He nodded to the half human, half refrigerator, who chewed gum noisily and did not respond as they sauntered by.

Braithwaite headed in the opposite direction, and Nige heard the sound of a car door closing and a vehicle pulling away, before the Cabin's door closed behind him. It was the first time he'd ever visited the place, the first time he'd ever indulged in something quite so downright *naughty*. Oh, he wasn't averse to backhanders or shady deals with unsavoury people, nor did he have any qualms about using prostitutes from time to time. But when Braithwaite had made contact with him about developing the old mine site, a project to which Potter had long been ideologically opposed, Nige had been surprised at how directly the old rogue had propositioned him.

'I can offer you the best whores outside of London,' Braithwaite had proclaimed, tongue curling unpleasantly around the words over the top of his wine glass. 'Hand-picked, and willing to do whatever you ask for.'

Nige had chosen his words carefully, imagining – as he always did – the conversation being played back later. The only way to survive in politics was to act like everyone was an undercover reporter, and to assume that nothing was ever, *ever*, off the record.

'Let's just say, purely hypothetically, that someone wanted to take advantage of such an offer. How might that progress?'

The purely hypothetical specifics had been hashed out over their fillet steaks. Nige's was medium rare, as it was supposed to be. Braithwaite's cremated portion looked almost as dust-dry and unappetising as the man himself.

And now, here Nige was. He had to admit, he was excited.

And all he had to do in return, in a few weeks' time when he'd won the Axton and Middlewich seat, was announce the development contract with Harrington and Braithwaite for the old mine site. *Only Braithwaite, now*, he realised, shuddering at the thought of the dead man's final moments, blood oozing out of his punctured belly as he expired like a stuck pig. No matter. If the Cabin was as stimulating as Braithwaite had promised, Nige envisaged a long and fruitful working relationship with the cadaverous ghoul.

And why shouldn't he take advantage of the meagre perks available in this shithole town? He understood why he'd been dumped here by the Party, that they considered his dynamism and comparative youth the perfect antidote to Potter's flabby, stalwart appeal. And he knew that once he secured the seat, he might have a route to a Cabinet position in a couple of reshuffles' time. But these facts didn't change how interminably godawful his existence was going to be until he could engineer an exit from this human septic tank, and from the legions of working-class no-hopers who wallowed in it.

At least the Cabin would provide him with a welcome and deserved distraction. The place was certainly sumptuously decorated. Outside it looked like a utilitarian log structure, but inside was all teak and mahogany, mounted deer heads and chandeliers made of antlers. The Italian – who had introduced himself, but whose name Nige had instantly forgotten – escorted him into a generously-proportioned living room, fitted with a bar at one end and a log fire burning pleasantly at the other.

Three lingerie-clad women were waiting for him on the L-shaped, tufted leather sofa. Nige paused in the doorway to eye them appreciatively, eyes bulging at the array of differently-coloured flesh on display.

And there's no need to worry about discretion, Braithwaite had intoned. *These girls won't sell your story to the papers, or do anything except dutifully service you.*

They know what will happen if they do.

He fixed them with his most charming smile, the one that melted the hearts of old ladies and convinced brainless yobs that he totally understood their hardships. They smiled back, one of them glancing coquettishly away, the others meeting his stare provocatively.

'Can I get you a drink?' asked the Italian.

'Ohh, I'm sure these ladies would love to share a bottle of champagne,' Nige replied with a wide grin. Then, under his breath, he hissed. 'It's on the house, right?'

'Of course,' replied his escort. 'Now why don't you make yourself comfortable while I fetch your drinks? I'll be only a minute, then I'll leave you all in peace to get to know each other.'

'To be honest, I'm not sure I can trust these girls to keep their hands off me for even that long,' said Nige, plonking himself down on the couch between two of the beauties, who giggled as though he'd delivered a hilarious quip.

'Oh, I'm sure they can be trusted to behave themselves,' the Italian chuckled. For a second, Nige thought he caught an edge to his tone, as if the words masked a veiled threat. He seemed to direct the sentence to one of the girls in particular, a beautiful pale creature perched on the corner of the wide settee, her demeanour perhaps a little less enthusiastic than the others.

Ahh, well. He wasn't there to reflect on their troubles. They were there to help him forget about his.

He started to unbutton his shirt, keen to get down to business.

32

IAN BRAITHWAITE

(OWNER AND CO-FOUNDER, HARRINGTON AND BRAITHWAITE PROPERTY GROUP)

I an sped towards the old mine. He'd called Bruno back three times, but the useless lump hadn't answered. His calls had gone to voicemail each time. *This is what you get for trusting pot-smoking morons, Ian.* He should have known better than to let past loyalties cloud his judgement. *A guard dog is no use once it's over the hill, no matter how faithful it is.*

Perhaps he should have assigned Vince to the job, but he didn't yet entirely trust the head of security. Then again, he didn't entirely trust anyone, a trait to which he owed his long life and relative prosperity. The point was, the gum-chewing meathead was John's hire, and this was a new era. It was time for the company to move past Harrington and his idiotic impulses. Siphoning money out of the business and back to Ian's associates in Russia would certainly be a lot easier now, too. No longer would he need to operate in the shadows, masking dividends as capital investments, burying questionable transactions amongst innocuous supplier payment runs. Threatening the head of the finance department with torture if he squealed about any of it. Harrington's death had been an unexpected liberation.

But still, it had been *unexpected*, and Ian did not like that. Not at all. His brain demanded control, at all times. Control of resources. Control of his carefully-crafted identity. Control of *people*. He scowled as he drove, the road unfurling darkly in front of him, as black and uncertain as the myriad possibilities that probed and gnawed at his mind.

Eric Potter had killed Harrington, because Harrington had been blackmailing him. Or at least, that's what the politician had claimed. Despite the ever-increasing size of his waistline, it didn't seem like something the old socialist would have the stomach for. But Ian didn't take chances. Potter would never believe that the extortion had been another of Harrington's private endeavours, another whim he'd indulged without consulting his business partner first.

Once again, Ian was left cleaning up John's mess.

A task he thought he'd delegated successfully. Bruno was supposed to have taken out Potter's representative, thereby sending the MP a clear message. *This is the big leagues, Eric, and you're not in any shape to compete.* But Bruno's infuriatingly cryptic phone call had not sounded encouraging, not at all.

I am sorry, Yuri. There has been... a big mistake.

He shuddered at the memory of his henchman's solemn tone. And for Bruno to use his real name... that detail unsettled him the most. Bruno might be a lazy pothead, but he was a smart man, and had once been a skilled soldier. He knew full well that the name 'Yuri' was a relic, an identity that even Ian's wife and daughter didn't know about. Something he'd sloughed off long ago, like an old skin.

He felt another surge of unhelpful, useless emotions at the thought of his wife. That alcoholic slut truly thought he didn't know she was sleeping with John behind his back. Did they both really think he was so stupid? That he wasn't maintaining the charade for the sake of his daughter? Poor Tammy... every time he saw those too-large, distended eyes staring back at him, he felt a surge of guilt. His ugliness, manifesting in her. As if nature had played a cruel genetic joke.

But he also saw in Tammy his other characteristics: his ruthlessness, his determination. The passion with which she'd thrown herself into her environmental activism, even if it brought her into direct conflict with him, had impressed her father. Maybe that was the whole reason she was doing it. Sometimes he couldn't tell if she respected him, or hated him.

Perhaps both.

She would inherit his business, one day, whether she wanted it or not.

He rounded the bend where the road would begin its familiar downward slope towards the mine. A blaze of red and blue lights greeted him, and he almost slammed his foot instinctively onto the brake pedal.

Bruno... what did you do?

He gently reduced his speed to something innocuous, slow enough for him to peer down the trail that led to the mine entrance as he drove past it, fast enough not to attract any attention. He could discern little on his drive-by, but could see that there were a large number of emergency service vehicles congregated there, maybe as many as eight. Squinting through the passenger window, he thought he saw a body bag being loaded into the back of one of the ambulances.

Fuck. This could only mean that there'd been a bloodbath. Bruno must have gotten himself arrested, or hopefully even into a shootout with the police. Ian had always been able to rely on Bruno not to spill any beans under interrogation, but it was yet another risk, another variable he could no longer control. Better if Bruno was lying dead on a stretcher, about to take a trip to the morgue.

For a moment he toyed with the idea of approaching, playing the 'I was just driving past the site because we're contemplating another bid to develop it, and couldn't help noticing all this commotion' card. But it was too perilous. As galling as it was, he was going to have to head back to the Cabin, and wait to see if Bruno phoned him back.

Unless I call Eric Potter, he thought. He removed one hand from the steering wheel and took out his phone, wondering whether the fat imbecile had engineered this outcome, or whether he had planned some scheme that had gone catastrophically awry. Then the device rang in his hand, and Ian almost cried out in surprise as he dropped it onto the passenger seat. He glanced at the screen, realising how jittery he was, how shaken by the flurry of unanticipated events over the last few days.

FIONA said the display. Why the hell was she calling him? He'd told her he was away on business all weekend. Maybe his words hadn't penetrated her prosecco-induced haze. He ignored it, using a layby to turn the car around. She called a second time while he was partway through the manoeuvre. What had gotten into her? He thought about picking up, wondering if it was some sort of emergency. Too many of them were competing for his attention that night.

But the prospect of talking to his wife was so unappealing that he couldn't bring himself to answer. *Fuck her, and fuck Potter.* He was going back to the Cabin. *Concentrate on what you can control.* As long as Nigel Hawke was enjoying himself, that was all that mattered. The Tory puke was going to win the election, and Ian would have the local council *and* the entire company entirely in his pocket. His associates would be most pleased at the sudden increase in his contributions to their cause.

Ian drove past the kaleidoscope of red and blue once again,

grunting with irritation as his phone informed him that Fiona had left a voicemail.

Ian Braithwaite's real name was Yuri Chebykin. He had moved to the UK in 1992 when he was in his late thirties, soon after the collapse of the USSR and the signature of numerous peace treaties with newly independent territories, such as Bruno's homeland of Latvia. This was an outcome Yuri had helped to facilitate. After all, communism was no good for business, no good for ambitious men who wanted, *craved*, the motivation that only wealth and success could provide. Communism made people the same, blended the exceptional with the mediocre, a great grotesque pestle and mortar that ground away aspiration and creativity and innovation and any desire except to exist, to work, to serve the homogenous whole.

When Vladimir Putin had succeeded Boris Yeltsin, Chebykin and his organisation had been happy to see the back of the vodka-swilling idiot. Putin's thirst for capitalist expansion had led the country to a boom period Chebykin had never thought he would witness. But, of late, things were souring. The democratic backslide, the dangerous interference in American politics, were worrying trends. The radiation poisoning of dissidents was even worse. Russia was beginning to seem more and more like a dangerous despotism, not a thriving marketplace.

And so his organisation's Machiavellian machinery, for so long dormant, was starting to rumble once more into life.

Machinery like that needed to be oiled, of course. Providing that lubricant was Chebykin's role. Ironically, he knew that some of his own people accused him of corruption, of putting his own decadent lifestyle with his blonde bimbo wife ahead of the group's best interests. Sometimes he wondered about them sending representatives to check up on him. It had taken a lot of very thorough background checks on Giacomo to satisfy him that the executive assistant was genuinely nothing more sinister than the unctuous subordinate he appeared to be.

But, if they *had* successfully inserted a mole into his camp, either that person hadn't yet found out about the Cabin, or else they'd chosen to turn a blind eye.

Ironically, Ian hated the place. He hated prostitutes, hated their diseases and sob stories, the way they used their bodies to prey upon men and then blamed them for the state of their own miserable lives. He hated his own weakness when he was attracted to them, a flaw he was determined not to act upon, unlike John, the reckless degenerate.

But the girls were a necessary evil, and the Cabin was the mechanism by which Ian could generate a return on their flesh. Like everything else, it was all machinery.

The house emerged from the darkness like a vision from a gothic horror story. He saw Hawke's BMW still outside, and breathed a sigh of relief. At least nothing had gone wrong with the politician's visit. Hawke would be a crucial ally in the coming months, barring an unforeseen disaster at the election. Unlocking the mine site was vital for H and B's growth plans. *H and B.* Ian wondered how soon was too soon to change the name, to expunge Harrington's involvement altogether. *Braithwaite Property Group* certainly had a nice ring to it.

He parked his car alongside the BMW, and started towards the door. It took him a few moments to realise Vince wasn't standing there. Ian stopped, frowning. With such a high-profile client inside, how could the numbskull have abandoned his post? Gritting his teeth, Ian marched towards the entrance, not wanting to call out the security guard's name in case he alarmed

Hawke, although his guest was hopefully far too distracted, enjoying his fill of champagne and female body parts.

He reached the door, and found it ajar. Acid frothed in his belly. It was bad enough to take a poorly-timed bathroom break, much worse to leave the place open and unguarded. Clearly his reservations about the masticating gorilla were well-founded. Seething, Ian pushed open the front door and stepped inside.

The first thing that struck him was the silence. There were no sounds of revelry, no loud music or clinking glasses, no nauseating sex noises from beyond the closed internal doors.

His second observation, microseconds later, was that his head of security was lying slumped against the hallway wall. Vince had sagged into an ungainly heap, his thick legs jutting out in front of him. His eyes and mouth were open, the piece of chewing gum still visible, trapped between his teeth and his lolling tongue.

Ian stared. Just like Harrington, Vince had suffered a stab wound to the abdomen. Just like Harrington, he had died with blood seeping from his belly into a spreading pool on the floor.

Ian's mouth felt as if every drop of moisture had been sucked out of it. He hovered there in the fashion of a confused insect, not knowing whether to venture further or to flee in terror. But what would he do after escaping? He couldn't exactly call the police to report the crime. Plus he'd have to find some way to dispose of the body... but before that he needed to know what the hell was going on. Where were Hawke and Giacomo?

His phone vibrated in his pocket, and he took it out to silence it, noticing once again that it was Fiona. Why the fuck did she keep calling him? His breath came in ragged, frightened gasps as he tried to recover his composure.

A thought pierced his brain, as sharp and deadly as the blade that had impaled his head of security. *What if this was*

Potter's doing? What if, somehow, the fat cretin had finally outmanoeuvred him? Perhaps the night's events were all connected: Bruno's unsettling message, Vince's grisly demise. His wife's phone calls.

New voicemail. Numbly, he lifted the phone to his ear.

For the first few seconds, all he could hear was sobbing. Then, Fiona's voice, twisted into an animal howl of anguish that penetrated the marrow of his bones.

'She's dead! Ian... somebody shot her... our baby's *dead...*'

The device clattered to the floor. Ian staggered, dazedly, towards the lounge.

This is a bad dream.

He reached towards the door handle, and pushed his way into the room as if he was drifting through layers of unreality.

You're about to wake up in your own bed next to your halfwit wife, with the whole day still ahead of you.

Beyond the door was a collection of images his brain refused to accept. He felt like his sanity was fraying, its final threads coming apart like the seams of some old clothing. He thought of Tammy's old childhood dresses, still in bags in the attic because Fiona refused to throw them away.

Unravelling.

At his feet, Giacomo knelt as though in supplication. The Italian was folded forwards like someone in prayer, his hands drawn inwards to his stomach. There was a wound in his back, which Ian at first thought meant he had been stabbed from behind, until he realised that a blade had simply been buried so deep in his assistant's belly that it had burst through the other side before being withdrawn. Thick blood oozed from both sides of the injury, spreading like treacle across the room's dark floorboards.

Ian stared vacantly down at Giacomo's kowtowing body until a sound drew his attention, and he glanced towards the bar. Nigel Hawke was standing there, completely naked, pressed up against the wood panelling like some offensive carving. His face was frozen into an expression somewhere between terror and disbelief. As with Giacomo, a dark pool was spreading beneath him, because Hawke had also been stabbed through the midsection. This time, though, the blade was still there, pinning him against the mahogany. It had passed through one of the hands the politician had raised to try to protect himself, fixing the outstretched palm in place in a gruesome freeze-frame. The other end of the blade was attached to a rifle.

The rifle was gripped by a figure in brown clothing.

The figure turned slowly towards him. Its eyes were wide and black and alien, its jaw tapering into a grotesque appendage resembling an elephant's trunk. A hard, perfectly-rounded skull, with some sort of monstrous protuberance around the circumference of its forehead.

A demon. The final strand of Ian's sanity threatened to snap.

Then he realised that what he was looking at wasn't some hellish monstrosity at all.

It was a man in a World War One uniform, complete with gas mask, helmet, and bayonet.

33

BRIAN CAULFIELD

(RETIRED BUSINESSMAN; RESIDENT OF BROOKHAVEN HALL)

B rian had watched them from the trees for a long time. At one point, he'd thought the lummox on the door had spotted him, perhaps catching the glint of the moonlight off his binoculars; but the appearance of Ian Braithwaite had distracted the bouncer. Brian had been there for a long time, assailed by the rain, feeling the cold gnawing malevolently at his old bones. But he knew he could not hope to succeed if he rushed things. So he waited, and he endured, observing the night's comings and goings like a watchman.

Like a soldier, on a mission.

He saw Braithwaite arrive, followed by the Mediterranean-looking man a while later, smoking one of those ridiculous fake cigarettes. Shortly after him, the black man in the trench coat had arrived, leaving his car somewhere down the trail and making the rest of the journey on foot. The man was now hiding in the trees opposite, presumably also watching the house, unaware that Brian was mirroring him from the other side of the building. The appearance of the man in the trench coat, and the nature of his involvement, was baffling. But it didn't deter Brian from his purpose.

Stephanie had told him that Nigel Hawke was going to be there tonight. Brian was there to kill him. Anyone who got in his way, including the mysterious observer, would have to be collateral damage.

Including the gum-chewing stooge on the front door, who had been a considerable challenge.

After Hawke had finally arrived, and Braithwaite had departed looking stressed and anxious, Brian had waited a long time for the big ape to leave his post. But everyone needed bathroom breaks, and Brian had had time on his side. He waited, and he watched, through the binoculars that had once been his grandfather's, as had everything else he was wearing and carrying. The uniform Benjamin Caulfield had worn proudly until he was hit by a speculative German round from an opposing trench. It hadn't been the bullet, but the infection, that had killed Brian's grandfather. Benjamin had died in a field hospital, surrounded by death and disease, immersed in the horrors of war. Horrors that today's youth knew nothing about, except what they saw in their bloody computer games.

Brian couldn't move as quickly as he used to, of course, so by the time he'd reached the front door, the oaf had already returned from his trip to the toilet. As the guard had opened the door, he'd found Brian standing on the opposite side. That had left Brian no choice but to skewer the bouncer where he stood, forcing the big man back inside and pinning him against the wall with the bayonet. He'd died slowly, wheezing and gasping, trying to speak but ending up almost choking on his chewing gum. No one had heard him. Music was playing, and the occasional whoops and giggles from the living room told Brian exactly where he'd find his true target.

The Mediterranean had surprised him, descending the stairs as he approached the source of the laughter, once again forcing Brian to stick him on the spot. The blade had snagged on one of his victim's ribs, and Brian had to force it violently through into the organs beyond, in the end pushing the man all the way backwards and through the door into the lounge. The man had struggled against his death, eventually collapsing to his knees with a mewl of horror and pain. Brian had to plant one foot on his shoulder in order to pull the blade out. At his side, the fire crackled and roared in the hearth, like an applauding audience.

A cry of terror came from his right. The squeal was emitted by Hawke, not by one of the girls that surrounded him. The politician was on the couch, along with a trio of women. All of them were naked. Brian blushed, scowling beneath the gas mask. Age was a strange curse, to be sure. The sight of women like that brought with it a weird concoction of excitement and guilt. Beautiful girls, whose soft flesh he couldn't pretend he wasn't interested in. But also girls young enough to be his granddaughters. Girls coerced and tricked into this shameful life. Girls like poor Stephanie, brought here by vile men like John Harrington. Another miscreant he'd watched through his grandfather's binoculars. Brian had hidden amongst the trees, soaked and quivering with anger, staring through the window while that lovely creature was made to perform indecencies on the old reprobate.

Even when he'd headed inside, carefully removing his boots so as not to leave muddy footprints throughout the care home, Brian hadn't known he meant to kill anyone. He'd started off merely watching people. Taking the binoculars with him on his midnight excursions. Sometimes he headed into town, skulking in the shadows, watching the drunks and the womanisers, hearing the foul language spewed into the air as though it was perfectly normal. Police trying to reason with these pieces of scum, these worthless hooligans.

At some point, he'd started taking the bayonet out with him.

He hadn't realised how easy the moment would be. The blade had slid into Harrington's fat belly like a carving knife into a Christmas turkey. The businessman had been petrified with horror, doing nothing to protect himself while Brian ruthlessly ended his depraved existence. Maybe it was the shock of the gas mask. Maybe the pain. But Brian fancied that, until that moment, John Harrington had begun to doubt his own mortality, just as all other arrogant rich fools do. Bezos and Musk and all the other egomaniacs on the news, fantasising about going to Mars, dreaming of technology that would enable them to live forever.

The fact that he'd disabused Harrington of such delusions made Brian intensely happy. Because no one is above the cold hand of death. Not Brian, not his grandfather, not his dad who'd died in the mines beneath the town, back when coal was Axton's lifeblood. Certainly not a bloated, rich scumbag who thought he could do whatever he pleased. Brian had watched him stagger back into his office, his own breath deafening inside the mask while the younger man gasped and groaned and finally fell silent. Then he'd walked calmly back to his room to change, frightening that poor old crackpot Mrs Vickers as he passed her in the corridor.

Hawke screamed again, reminding Brian of where he was, and that he still had work to do. He advanced towards the sofa, the girls scattering immediately.

'I'm only here for him,' Brian shouted, pointing the rifle and its blood-drenched blade straight at Hawke's black heart. 'Please make your way out, quietly.' He didn't want to frighten them. 'And take your clothes – you'll catch your death of cold out there.' He wasn't sure if they could hear him from beneath the mask, but one of them seemed to take charge, a pale girl who encouraged the others to grab some items from behind the sofa and then led them away, skirting the perimeter of the room as though Brian was a bomb about to go off. He ignored them as they fled, keeping his eyes fixed on Hawke in case the scrawny weasel tried anything. It seemed unlikely. Hawke had wet himself, voiding his bladder onto the leather sofa like a weakling child. Contempt twisted Brian's expression as he observed the trembling, quaking figure before him.

'Please,' the politician said. 'Please don't hurt me. What have I even done?'

Brian said nothing. He just stared, and breathed through the mask, feeling anger surging through his old veins. It made him feel alive. Like a drug. Maybe he was no better than some of these hedonists. Maybe he deserved to die, too.

'Please,' Hawke whimpered. 'Please just let me go.'

'Stand up,' Brian hissed. 'Get up against the bar.'

Hawke scrambled to his feet and moved towards the wooden structure, obediently pressing himself against it. His flesh was pasty, his body as skinny as a scarecrow. His cock seemed to have disappeared entirely, retracted into the tangle of his red pubic hair. The man who was supposed to take Axton into the new decade. The man who Brian had been planning to vote for.

'Please,' Hawke said again, sobbing.

A deviant and a philanderer. Brian thought of Stephanie, used and abused by these powerful men, these corrupt patriarchs. He thought of all the words he could use to express his revulsion, his disappointment. He thought about his arguments with Owen, how everything got muddled up between them, politics and the world and his own fears and regrets. He thought about how he wanted to tell his son he loved him, but never could, never would.

Instead, he drove the bayonet into Hawke with the fury of a man half his age.

The politician hung there, like a rare moth pinned to a piece of balsa wood. He gave one long, gurgling breath as his life seeped out of him, spurting blood pooling around Brian's feet. He hadn't bothered to take his boots off this time. He didn't really care if he was caught. What did it matter? Owen looked at him with naked disdain on the rare occasions he even visited, and his other child never spoke to him at all.

'My grandfather died because of people like you,' Brian spat. 'People who went to war willingly, all so you could sign your treaties, and drink your wine, and sleep around behind your wives' backs.' He twisted the blade, which had passed through Hawke's extended hand, and watched the politician gasp and squirm in agony. 'You aren't fit to govern this country. None of you are.'

Then the door opened, and Ian Braithwaite stumbled into the room.

Brian withdrew the bayonet, and Hawke crumpled to the floor in a wheezing, gargling heap. He turned towards the businessman, hatred blazing in his guts as he advanced towards him. This man was another who needed to be purged, the architect of so much misery. Another fiend that had poured poison into the ears of his precious Stephanie.

'Wait,' said the newcomer, holding up his spindly hands. He seemed dazed, a man half-sleepwalking. 'You... you killed John Harrington, didn't you?'

Brian didn't need to reply. Soon this insect was going to be twitching at the end of his bayonet. He didn't owe him any explanation at all. But he nodded, wanting the slimeball to know that the moment of his final reckoning had arrived.

'I thought so,' Braithwaite replied, surprisingly unfazed.

'Did you kill my fucking daughter as well?' At this Brian halted, confused. He shook his head.

'I don't know what's happening,' the tycoon said, falteringly. He looked down at Giacomo's genuflecting corpse. 'Everything has suddenly... come apart.' Brian realised that tears had formed in the dusty crevices of Braithwaite's eyes. An urge took hold of Brian, and he reached up with one hand to remove his helmet. Next, he tugged off the gas mask, letting both fall to the floor. Braithwaite stared into his face, a face older even than his own. Brian wondered what he saw there, whether he could see the rage burning in its rheumy eyes. The face of an old man.

Or the face of his judge and executioner.

'Who are you?' Braithwaite whispered, his face creasing with bewilderment. Brian said nothing. 'Is this about money?' the tycoon snapped. 'I can give you money. I've got a hundred grand in a safe, back at Brookhaven. The code is written here!' The businessman reached into the pocket of his coat and extracted a folded slip of paper. 'John, that worm, had been hiding it from me. You did me a favour by killing him. Come on, you and I don't need to be enemies! You can just take this code, go and get the money, and go wherever you want. I won't tell a soul.'

Brian stepped forwards, reaching out a hand. Braithwaite handed the note to him. Brian glanced at it, then screwed it up and let it fall to the floor. 'With you people, it always comes down to money,' he snarled, gesturing at Hawke, now a pitiful heap behind him. 'It's the essence of your lives, the only motivation you can comprehend. Well, hard as it may be for you to believe it, some of us don't care about money. Some of us care about *morality*.' He spat at Braithwaite's feet. The businessman stared, incredulous, as Brian raised the bayonet.

Planting his feet, Brian thrust the weapon forwards, as he'd done four times previously, as he'd seen people do countless times in the war films and documentaries he loved so much. This time, though, the blade did not sink into the yielding flesh of his enemy. This time his adversary was too quick, darting to one side and crouching to snatch up the iron poker that was propped next to the fireplace. Brian turned, with the sluggishness of a man wearing a cumbersome uniform, with the weariness of a man in his late seventies. He managed to raise the rifle to block Braithwaite's swinging blow, but the impact staggered him, driving him to one knee.

'You stupid idiot,' Braithwaite fumed. 'Now, if you know anything about what happened to my daughter, you'd better tell me, or I'll cave your head in!' His voice was half entreaty, half incandescent fury. The businessman raised the poker, bulbous eyes as wide and yellow as pickled eggs.

'All I know about your daughter,' Brian rasped, 'is that she deserves a better father than you.'

He surged to his feet, all of his remaining strength forced downwards into his ancient joints, propelling him upright and into the air in a leaping spring that carried him into Braithwaite and sent the two of them crashing into the fireplace. The bayonet, useless at this range, clattered to the ground behind him as the two of them sprawled amongst the burning logs. Braithwaite clung grimly to the poker, Brian trying to wrestle it from his hands as flames licked at his uniform.

The businessman was thinner and scrawnier than Brian, but he was also fifteen years his junior. Shrieking as the fire scalded his flesh, the younger man managed to wriggle free from Brian's grasp, rolling away from the blaze and batting frantically at his smouldering clothes with his free hand. Brian struggled to his feet, ready for Braithwaite to launch another attack with the poker. He could smell the singeing of his own outfit, could see that the flames were spreading rapidly around him, leaping hungrily from the burning logs that had split onto the floorboards, dancing across the nearby tablecloth and the wall hangings. He bent, wincing, and scooped up one of the firebrands.

If the night was to end in an inferno, so be it.

He moved forwards, swinging the log in a clumsy arc that Braithwaite was able to deftly sidestep once again. Brian felt the poker crack against his lower back, and dropped to his knees, wincing with pain and frustration, waiting for another blow to connect with his skull, to put an end to his crusade.

'Stop!' shouted a voice from the doorway. As one, Brian and Braithwaite turned towards its source: it was the black man in the long camel-coloured trench coat, the one who he'd seen sneaking into the grounds earlier that night. 'You're going to burn the bloody place down!' Brian saw that the man was carrying a weapon, a snub-nosed revolver that was aimed into the room but currently at neither man, his allegiances perhaps as yet undecided.

'Who the fuck are *you*?' shouted Braithwaite.

'An interested party,' the man replied. 'I've been watching this place all night. I saw you go in.' He faced Brian. 'Then I saw the girls run away into the woods. Next, I saw the flames. I thought someone might need help.'

'Yes, *me*!' screeched Braithwaite. 'This nutcase is trying to kill me! Look, I don't care who you are – help me get out of this, and I'll give you *a hundred grand in cash*. I've got it hidden in a safe here in town. All you have to do is shoot this doddering lunatic, and we can go and get it, right now. But we need to get out of here before the whole place goes up!'

The man in the trench coat stared at Braithwaite for a long moment, as though considering his offer. Then he turned to Brian, and raised his pistol.

'Why did you do it?' he asked. 'Why did you kill Harrington, and these others?'

The man's dark eyes flickered with the reflected light of the flames, which were chewing through the room's furnishings like starving rodents.

'I couldn't stand it anymore,' Brian said, still on his knees, coughing as the billowing smoke seeped into his lungs. 'Watching them prey on people. I realised there'd be no justice for them, not unless I dispensed it myself.'

'You can't just kill people you don't agree with.'

'*Yes you can*,' Brian snapped. 'That's the whole point. That's what my granddad did, in the First World War. That's what our boys did when we stood up to Hitler. Sometimes violence is the only answer.' He felt suddenly very, very tired. A great, hot wave of exhaustion swept over him, his vision darkening as though someone had tossed a warm blanket over his head. 'This world is diseased,' he managed to continue, jabbing a gloved finger towards Braithwaite. 'And these men are the cancer. Cancers need to be cut out.' He swayed on his knees, almost toppling forwards. The burning log clattered to the ground next to him.

'What are you waiting for?' Braithwaite implored the man in the trench coat. His voice seemed distant and faint. 'Shoot him!'

People were all the same. *Everybody has a price.* Brian closed his eyes, awaiting the moment of his death. It felt in some ways like a relief. 'If you're going to shoot me,' he slurred, 'then shoot me. I hope the money makes it all worthwhile.'

Seconds moved sluggishly, like centuries, like lifetimes. Like a world, moving on.

The gun did not go off.

'No one's killing anyone,' he heard the main in the trench coat say, as though hearing it from inside a dream. 'Not unless either of you tries anything. Now I want both of you to walk out of here, before—'

The man in the trench coat never finished the sentence, because with a deafening creak, a splitting and cracking noise like the sound of some colossal wooden golem being cleaved in two, the roof above them sagged suddenly downwards. A thick beam of wood was disgorged like a piece of splintered bone, falling onto the man and knocking him to the ground. He was pinned, helpless, beneath the smouldering chunk, his pistol tumbling from his hands.

Brian stared at the gun for several moments, knowing what he needed to do, unable to compel his body and brain into obedience. Moving groggily, he tried to haul himself to his feet, but Braithwaite was faster. The tycoon aimed a vicious kick into Brian's face, and at last the darkness at the edges of Brian's vision swarmed inwards to claim him.

34

URSULA PEMBRIDGE

(DETECTIVE SERGEANT, CHESHIRE CONSTABULARY)

F riedel updated Ursula on the condition of the man he'd
apprehended as she sped towards the blaze. The DI was
furious that the station hadn't notified them of the emergency
call from the mine, and a lone constable had instead been
dispatched to the site. By the time Friedel had arrived, the scene
was a disaster: an injured police officer, a dead girl, and a killer
who'd almost managed to blow his own head apart until Friedel
rugby-tackled him. The four other youths Friedel and the
supporting officers had rescued from the tunnels didn't have a
clue what was going on, but confirmed that they'd been the ones
to call 999 when they saw bodies being dumped into the
collapsed shaft.

'I failed that girl,' said Friedel, who'd been staking out the
construction site, sensing that the AEM's planned act of
vandalism might link somehow to the case. His hunch had been
right; just not his location.

Ursula, meanwhile, had been following up on the address
Friedel had taken from the contract on Harrington's desk.
Hunting for an old hikers' rest stop in the woods after dark had
felt like a waste of time, but Friedel had been insistent that they

202

split up to pursue both leads. She'd been driving grumpily around the perimeter of the forest when she'd stumbled upon an old, well-hidden dirt trail, close to the site of an automobile accident earlier that day. It had led her deep into the densely-knotted trees, and at first she'd expected it to peter out into an impassable, overgrown dead end.

Instead, she'd seen the flames.

'You can't think like that,' she told him. 'There's no way we could have known they'd switch locations. Or that there'd be a mad gunman waiting there for them when they got there.'

'I should have anticipated they'd go somewhere else after you grilled that boy in the coffee shop.'

'Not "I",' she said sternly. '"*We.*" We're a team, remember?' Friedel fell silent. 'Anyway, put your foot down and get here as quickly as you can – something's going on. There's a fire, right in the middle of the forest.'

'What?'

She explained how to find the dirt track, although as she drew nearer to the worsening conflagration, she realised he would probably see the flames from a long way away.

'I'll be maybe ten minutes,' he promised.

The blaze was growing rapidly, and she began to worry it would spread to the surrounding woodland. Her next call was to the fire brigade; she didn't want the nightmare evening to end with Axton engulfed in a forest fire. As concisely as possible, she explained where she was and what was going on, and that multiple fire engines and ambulances might be needed.

Then she was forced to end the call abruptly, because a trio of barely-clothed women emerged suddenly from the trees, directly in front of her. She crunched the brakes, swerving to a halt, and leapt out of the vehicle.

After she'd convinced them that she was a police detective, the women reluctantly agreed to join Ursula in the car. The thought of being taken back to the place from which they had just fled was clearly far from appealing, but the prospect of getting lost in the forest, not to mention the abject unsuitability of their attire for such a bitterly cold evening, had helped her persuade them to climb into the back of the vehicle. They were terrified and shaken, but had been able to explain that their names were Elira, Irene and Gabby, and that there had been others in the burning building, which was apparently known as 'the Cabin'.

They'd been entertaining a client when a terrifying man with a bayonet had burst in, wearing a gas mask and a military uniform, and stabbed one of the staff to death. The security guard was dead too; they'd run past his body in the hallway as they fled. As far as they knew, that left only the client and his attacker still inside. The killer had been threatening the client with the weapon when he'd granted them their escape.

That has to be the same man that killed Harrington, Ursula thought. She mashed her foot against the accelerator, hurtling towards the roaring blaze that waited beyond the trees like an enraged demon. Seconds later, the trail suddenly flattened out into a wide clearing. At its centre was a large wooden house, so completely aflame it looked as if it had attracted the wrath of a deity.

This must be the address in the woods, she thought. *But what the hell is going on here?*

She stopped the car, staring up at the wreckage of the building as it was swallowed by the flames.

Hell is right.

She leapt out of the vehicle, hurrying towards the inferno, past the other four cars that were gathered outside. Mercifully, they and the surrounding trees were far enough away that they hadn't yet caught fire. She didn't know what she hoped to achieve – entering a burning building was suicide, and she didn't even know if either of the men were still inside. But she had a chance to apprehend the murderer, to close the case and repair some of the evening's chaos. She hurried onwards, squinting into the flames. Even at this distance, the heat was overwhelming.

Suddenly, a figure appeared in the doorway.

'Hey!' she cried. 'Hey, come this way!'

The figure was a man, old and grey-haired, but it was difficult to make out any other specifics so close to the violent glow. He paused under the crumbling porch, staring at her.

'Quickly!' she shouted, rushing towards him and waving her hands. 'It's going to collapse!'

He raised his arm. At first Ursula thought he was signalling for help, and that the bang she heard was the sound of a gas canister or aerosol can exploding inside the building behind him. She only realised what was happening when a bullet whizzed past her cheek.

What in God's name?

She veered sideways as another gunshot boomed above the sound of the fire, then another. There was no cover in the clearing whatsoever – her only chance was to keep moving, zigzagging her way towards the tree line to her left. A fourth bullet smacked into the ground inches in front of her, spraying wet earth into the air.

As she tried once again to change direction, the fifth bullet caught her in the calf, and Ursula collapsed to the ground with a shocked yelp of pain. Clutching her wounded leg, she rolled onto her back in time to see her assailant striding calmly towards her across the open ground. Behind him, the flames danced and roared as though he was some evil pyromancer straight out of a fantasy movie.

But this was no warlock, and there was no magic at work here. A demon perhaps, but only in the metaphorical sense. The man approaching her, aiming a snub-nosed revolver at her face, was Ian Braithwaite.

'You'll be in a lot more trouble if... if you kill me,' Ursula breathed, the pain in her leg almost unbearable. She was pretty sure the bullet had passed straight through the flesh, but in that moment such a fragment of good luck didn't help her much at all. She couldn't get up, and her blood seeped between her fingers as she stared up at the old businessman, whose hair had been whipped into a frenzy by the wind. The billowing grey strands and his bulging eyes made him look maniacal, something not quite human.

'My daughter is dead,' he hissed malevolently. 'Do you think I give a shit about you, or anyone else? And besides, you're completely wrong: if I kill you, no one will know I was even here.' His half-crazed, death's head grin contained not a sliver of mirth. 'Everything linking me to this place is either being burnt to a crisp in there, or will be shredded as soon as I've cleared out John's office. Your death will be blamed on the man who owned this gun, who's currently squashed under a fallen ceiling back in there...' He gestured nonchalantly over his shoulder. The Cabin spewed fire into the air, underscoring his point. '... Or on the lunatic who killed John Harrington, who I suspect might die of old age before the fire cooks him.' Braithwaite glanced disdainfully at the weapon in his hand. 'I thought about executing them both, you know, but I'm glad I didn't bother. Otherwise I wouldn't have had enough bullets left to finish you off.'

He pointed the gun at her head. Ursula tried to haul herself to her feet, but only succeeded in lifting her skull closer to the barrel. Still she stared up at him, refusing to close her eyes, refusing to give him the satisfaction of seeing her submit. Behind him, the burning building looked like it was coughing up the contents of the Earth's core.

Then a shape careered into Braithwaite, the gun knocked from his grasp moments before it went off. The bullet disappeared uselessly into the starless night sky as Braithwaite crashed into the mud, pinned to the ground by three attackers who scratched and gouged and bit at him as he struggled.

'What the fuck are you doing?' he shrieked, as Elira, Irene and Gabby held him down.

'Shut up,' snapped Elira, raking her fingernails across his face. Braithwaite screamed in pain.

Ursula dragged herself into a sitting position, reaching for her PAVA spray. 'I suggest you stop struggling,' she said, aiming the burning liquid at Braithwaite's eyes. He seemed to recognise what it was, and fell still, trembling with pain and rage.

'Thank you,' Ursula said to the women that had saved her life. 'My colleague should be here in–'

The sound of an approaching vehicle interrupted her, and she turned towards the trees. An unmarked car burst into the clearing, skidding to a halt close to her own. She watched with a half-smile as DI Friedel leapt out of the driver's seat.

'Over here!' she shouted. 'I'm okay... but I need an ambulance.'

She returned her gaze to Braithwaite as her colleague sprinted towards her, not wanting to give the murderous bastard a chance to try anything. But Braithwaite remained subdued and helpless on the ground. The scratches on his face glowed a livid red; Ursula didn't intend to mention them in her report.

She felt a spot of water on her face, followed by another. Beyond Braithwaite, the building blazed, too far gone to be saved by the rain. She watched it burn, waiting for the disintegrating structure to finally give way and collapse into itself.

Then she saw movement, beneath the sagging porch.

'How are you feeling? Still hate my guts?'

Friedel had used torn strips of his jacket to craft a makeshift tourniquet, yanking it so tight that she'd threatened him with violence.

'Nahh,' she replied. 'Although I wish you'd been the one to go and check out the address in the woods.'

She'd blacked out on her way to the hospital, and awoken to find herself in a bed with her wound dressed and a doctor standing over her.

'They didn't need to operate on your leg?'

She shook her head. 'The bullet missed the bone, thankfully. It should heal up okay. But I might have to give up the netball for a while.' Friedel smiled, but she saw sadness in his eyes. 'What's up?'

'The old man didn't make it,' he replied.

'Ahh, shit,' she said. The man had collapsed in the doorway of the burning building seconds after Friedel's arrival. Despite his age, he'd somehow managed to carry the large frame of the other survivor on his back. 'Any idea who he is yet?'

Friedel nodded. 'His son was with him when he died. His name was Brian Caulfield, one of the residents of Brookhaven.' He paused, chewing his lip. 'He might be our killer, Ursula.'

'What?' She jerked into a sitting position, feeling immediately dizzy and lying back down with a grimace at the pain in her leg.

'He was wearing an old military uniform, and we've recovered a World War One bayonet from the scene. There were three other bodies inside, all badly burned, all awaiting identification. But I think he used that same weapon to kill them all, and John Harrington too. Can you believe it? A 78-year-old serial killer.'

'What about the other survivor?' The old man had rescued a black man in a long trench coat from the scene.

'He'll live. We're still waiting for him to wake up, though. He's in a pretty bad way after part of the ceiling collapsed on him.'

'Any idea who he is yet?'

Friedel nodded. 'He's a Private Investigator named Patrick Ademola. He had his ID with him. It might even have been his gun that Braithwaite shot you with.'

Braithwaite. Ursula shuddered as she remembered his sneering face, his snakelike voice. The callousness with which he'd been about to end her life. 'So what's happened to that piece of work?'

Friedel shrugged. 'There's a lot to unravel here. I'm hoping the detective will know more. But it seems likely Harrington and Braithwaite were using that building to run some sort of prostitution racket. Entertaining high-profile clients, that sort of thing. You won't believe the photos we've recovered from Braithwaite's car.'

She raised an inquisitive eyebrow. When he told her, she raised the other too.

'Jesus. This could get political.'

'Yeah. And I don't do politics.'

'Has Braithwaite confessed to anything?'

Friedel shook his head. 'He's got some big shot Russian lawyer with him. But we might not need him. The man I arrested at the mine appears to be in the mood to talk.' Friedel paused again. 'It was Braithwaite's daughter. The dead girl I found in the tunnel.'

Ursula exhaled slowly. 'Shit. What, a professional hit?'

Friedel shook his head. 'A freak accident, apparently. The shooter feels so guilty about it that he's answering everything we ask him. Like he's desperate to get it all off his chest.'

'Have they recovered any bodies from the collapsed mineshaft yet?'

Friedel paused, shaking his head as though in disbelief. 'Cherries,' he said.

'Err... I'm sorry?' Ursula wondered if she'd dreamed the entire conversation.

'The synaesthesia,' he said. 'You remember I was telling you how emotions have a taste? Well, cherries is what astonishment tastes like.'

'What do you mean?' She felt a strange mixture of excitement and unease swelling within her.

'We haven't recovered the bodies yet, but the shooter has told us who one of them is. And he's already been confirmed as missing by his wife.'

'Who?'

Friedel shook his head again. 'Brace yourself. This is going to get *really* political.'

CODA
JOHN HARRINGTON (DECEASED)

John Harrington watched them talk. He didn't watch them in the conventional sense, because John Harrington was dead. However, he had learned since his demise that dead people continue to exist, after a fashion. Except he hadn't learned it, not really, because learning suggests a logical chronology, a structured order of events whereby something happens, and you remember it, enabling you to apply its teachings when similar situations arise in the future.

In Limbo, there was no past or future. Only an endless, lukewarm now.

You couldn't learn from your mistakes when you were unable to compose complex thoughts, because every attempt fragmented and seeped away like liquid on a polished surface. You couldn't apply the accumulated wisdom of your life when no situations arose in which to utilise it; no interactions, no quandaries, no dilemmas or threats or opportunities.

In Limbo, there was no scenery. No other people. No joy, or pain, no delight or suffering. No pity. No guilt. No repentance. Just a constellation of consciousnesses, hanging there as though pinned in place, each utterly oblivious to the next. Each one was a desolate star, haunted by its nebulous memories. Dark voids within a dark void.

John Harrington had nothing to do but watch.

He saw them, scurrying far beneath him like insects, like bacteria, like charged electrons. The stuff of which the universe was made. He also saw them up close, as he swooped through the streets and the trees like a ghost, borrowing their eyes and ears to experience each moment, every moment, all at once. An ocean of events and thoughts and feelings swept through him, while he felt almost nothing. They crashed against his dispassion like waves against a barren beach.

Yet some moments stuck out, lighthouses in the dark expanse.

He saw the firefighters battling the hellish blaze as the Cabin was consumed, saw them successfully prevent the flames from spreading to the parked cars or the surrounding trees. He saw Elira Neziri, along with Irene and Gabby – the three women that had entertained the Cabin's VIP that night – sheltering at the police station where they'd been given fresh clothes and hot coffee. But because time was condensed in Limbo, the chain of causality broke down, its discrete steps merged and melted like a chain of pearls tipped into a furnace. This meant John Harrington could also see their futures. Like diamonds, they emerged, whole and flawless, from the crushed and compacted chaos of their lives.

Irene and Gabby quickly found their way back to an approximation of their old existence. They didn't have the spirit to break away from it; it was all they'd known for so many years. Neither lived long. They were alongside John, somewhere, hovering in the void. He was not sad, or smug, about this. There were no such feelings in Limbo.

Elira, on the other hand, was helped by a charity that supported women in her situation. She was able to secure UK citizenship, and to start her own business. She was assisted in her endeavours by Camilla, whose artistic talents were the foundation of their interior design company, and the two of them rarely spoke of their shared past, or their suffering at the hands of Ricky Cox.

Cox himself recovered from the injuries inflicted upon him by Harry Torrance, but committed suicide a few years later. Both men's consciousnesses had also been subsumed into the abyss. Many others had joined them since John's passing: Vince Reynolds, the security guard John had hired, whose brutality had once so impressed him; Nigel Hawke and Eric Potter, the politicians for whom the seat of Axton and Middlewich no longer held anything more than a vague, ethereal memory; Giacomo Esposito, John's executive assistant, whom he and his business partner had treated little better than garbage; Tammy Braithwaite, Ian's own daughter, an innocent life cut tragically short.

Brian Caulfield was identified as the killer of four men: John Harrington, Vince Reynolds, Giacomo Esposito and Nigel Hawke. The discovery of the latter caused a huge political stir, even greater than the recovery of Eric Potter's body from the old mine site, with both major parties accusing each other of sleaze and corruption. Following the scandal, as well as the deaths of his father and his boss, Owen Caulfield reflected on his career and his politics, and decided to leave the Labour Party.

He joined the campaign of an independent candidate, Jade Derbyshire, who became the youngest ever MP when she won the Axton and Middlewich seat in a landslide victory, after it was eventually contested following a four-month delay. She dedicated her campaign to her murdered friend, Tammy, delivering a two-pronged message of anti-corruption and environmental responsibility. Lewis Jones and Collin Taylor also worked on her campaign team, while Ayesha Kumari decided that politics and activism weren't for her, although she and Collin went on to enjoy a decades-long relationship. Jade's election meant that the mine remained an area of natural beauty, never sold to developers during her tenure, although it was forever tainted by the events of that rain-soaked night.

Others had avoided death, albeit only affording themselves a sliver of time in the grand scheme of things (although there was no grand scheme, no intelligence behind any of this – just the inscrutable machinations of a universe that didn't care who lived or died or wept or suffered). Ian Braithwaite was originally charged with pimping offences, but the police investigation into his affairs soon yielded many more crimes. Among them was his involvement in the murders of several women, whose remains were discovered when the woodland around the Cabin was searched.

Harrington watched impassively as Braithwaite spent his remaining years in prison, tortured by the memory of his daughter, and the knowledge of his complicity in her fate. One secret that Braithwaite did manage to take to his grave was his involvement with the shadowy Russian organisation he'd always worked for. They quietly washed their hands of him, and pursued alternative sources of funding and political leverage.

Ian Braithwaite's wife, Fiona, did not visit her husband once in prison. She lived a deeply unhappy life for several more years, before dying of alcohol poisoning.

John beheld a better future for PC Zack Wozniak, who recovered from his broken ribs and internal bleeding. He achieved the rank of DI, working alongside Ursula Pembridge under Tobias Friedel, who replaced Abigail McKenzie as DCI in the coming years. After taking down Ian Braithwaite, the group investigated and cracked many other difficult cases together.

Bruno Berzins, the former soldier and odd job man whom

Braithwaite had deployed to undertake his dirty work, also survived. He went to prison for the murder of Tammy Braithwaite, and was haunted by the memories of what he had done, and by the knowledge that he had let down his employer as well as his family. Monica, his wife, visited him dutifully, although like his former boss, he passed away before he was released to her.

Patrick Ademola, too, was spared. Thanks to Brian Caulfield, he recovered from his injuries and the damage done by smoke inhalation, and continued to run his private investigation business. He was helped by Kim Harrington, who insisted on paying him five times what they'd agreed for cracking the safe. After all, he'd done exactly what she'd wanted: he'd burnt the Cabin to the ground.

Kim had plenty of money to spare, as she'd inherited John's half of the business under the rules of intestacy, despite the absence of any will. John observed this with the same cool detachment as he perceived everything else. She sold it immediately, and donated much of the remaining proceeds to the charity for which she continued to work.

H and B was ultimately broken up. Although Yvette Morris was one of many people who lost their jobs, she became a successful project director for her new employers, continuing to ensure that disabled access was top of their agenda in all their building projects. She recruited Leannah Ryan to work for her, who dumped Wayne Morgan after finding out that he'd started cheating on her. Wayne continued to work at the Silver Birch for many years, full of regret and failed ambition, never achieving his dreams of becoming a chef.

Despite being sold off as part of the H and B asset portfolio, Brookhaven Hall continued to run for many more years. The care home's new owners promoted Marie Derbyshire to General Manager, replacing Bex Catterall, who decided to pursue a new career as a veterinary surgeon. Greg Tapson kept his job, and kept in touch with his two sons while raising his new, healthy daughter. Mrs Vickers, Brookhaven's oldest resident, lived to be over a hundred years old, still constantly talking about her son Robbie, who continued to visit her every week. She appreciated this, even if she often got confused, or forgot his visits had happened as soon as he'd left.

To Mrs Vickers, like John Harrington, time no longer worked in the familiar sense.

John Harrington's glacial gaze swept across the town, past the Middlewich Hotel and Spa where Nicolas Muñoz continued to work, even after the place sold out and became a Premier Inn. It drifted over the pothole in Penelope Stroud's road, which the local council eventually fixed after she complained in person to Jade Derbyshire MP. It moved emotionlessly across the form of Dawn Potter, sleeping alone, crying quietly at her husband's graveside, staring at pictures of the two of them smiling together and wondering how many times he had slept with other women behind her back.

It settled, as it often did, on the trees, where animals still gnawed at each other's bones, and at the bones of badly-buried corpses. John wondered if those trees watched the atrocities, the ups and downs and trials and tribulations, the petty concerns and squabbles and ambitions and paranoia with which Axton was permeated. The town's secrets, as tangled and entrenched as rusted chains, as ancient roots.

He wondered if the trees had dreams and fears of their own. If they each had a different perspective on what they witnessed, an unshakeable idea of how the universe should operate and how stupid and intolerable every other viewpoint was.

Or perhaps they merely watched, thoughtless and empty, very different from the human beings with whom they shared the world.

EPILOGUE

STEPHANIE GLEBE (CARE WORKER, BROOKHAVEN
HALL)

S tephanie hurried past the room, trying not to glance into it.
She knew it would only make her sad. Even though he'd
been dead for nearly a week, it was still very much Brian's room,
the old man's collection of military paraphernalia and patriotic
knick-knacks still adorning the walls and every available surface.
A family member was due to come and collect them at some
point, but she understood why they might need time. She wasn't
even related to the dead man – in fact, she'd barely known him
at all, it seemed, given what she'd found out about him since the
destruction of the Cabin – but she still missed him terribly. The
thought of scooping all that stuff into boxes or bin bags, of
sealing up sacks of memories and tossing them into the tip, must
be heartbreaking. It would certainly break hers.

And her heart was not in a position to withstand much more
damage. Dan had punched her two nights previously, after the
police had been round for a second time to ask questions. He
hadn't been present when she'd been questioned about the
Cabin and her involvement in its sordid entertainments, but it
had been all over the news, and for all his faults Dan wasn't a
complete idiot.

Brothel burns on night of bloodshed

Politicians slaughtered as secret Axton prostitution ring exposed

He'd come home drunk and outright accused her of being involved, and when she'd tried to deny it he'd swung a right hook into her cheek. For a moment he'd seemed almost as surprised as she'd been; but even as she blinked in shock, finding herself suddenly on the floor with pain exploding around the still-black eye she'd since done her best to mask with make-up, he hadn't apologised, hadn't volunteered any remorse for what he'd done. The blow was like a promise, a silent guarantee that there was more violence to come if she didn't confess to him. Perhaps worse, when and if she did.

He'd stood over her while she struggled to her feet, staring vengefully into her eyes as she pushed past him on her way to lock herself in the bathroom. She'd hidden there for hours until he was finally asleep.

The previous night she'd been at work, mercifully. Maybe she could just work every night, forever. She knew she had to leave him. But how could she? Without the extra money from working at the Cabin her finances would be in worse shape than ever. She didn't even have a separate bank account.

She realised her hands were shaking and decided to head to the kitchen for a cup of tea. Thankfully Marie was on shift with her again that night, which at least meant she didn't have to face another grilling from Greg Tapson. Her life felt as if it had become a series of interrogations: by the police, by Dan, by her work colleagues, even by a reporter who'd turned up at Brookhaven earlier that week, and been told in no uncertain terms by Marie where he could stick his interview.

Everyone wanted to know what she'd done. But the last

time she'd opened up to someone, she knew what had happened. She'd told Brian, and because of her, he and others had died that very same night.

It's not your fault, she told herself as she poured hot water from the kettle. *You didn't make him into a murderer. He was just a crazy old man. You shouldn't feel guilty, and you shouldn't miss him so much.* But she did, nonetheless. Perhaps if her dad hadn't died when she was so young, things would have worked out differently. Perhaps Brian had been a sort of twisted version of a father figure. *Perhaps perhaps perhaps. Perhaps you've got to accept the way life is, and stop feeling sorry for yourself.*

She glanced out of the window, remembering the creature she'd seen, out in the woods with its gigantic eyes. She'd thought it was an alien, a bug-eyed monster. Now she knew it had been Brian, wearing his gas mask, watching her. The thought made her shiver, and when the doorbell sounded she jumped, losing her grip on the cup of tea. It fell to the floor and shattered, spraying hot liquid and ceramic fragments around her feet.

'Oh, love, what's gotten into you?' said Marie, appearing in the kitchen doorway. 'Just leave that, I'll clean it up for you. But let me get the door first. If it's that reporter again I'll shove his notepad up his arse myself.'

'It's okay, Marie,' Stephanie replied, forcing her nerves under control. 'I'll get it. I need to face things myself. If you don't mind cleaning up this mess, I'll make you a brew in a sec.'

'It's a deal,' Marie said, bustling towards the cupboard where the dustpan and brush were kept. Stephanie felt another pang of guilt; Marie had also survived a week from hell. Her own daughter, hunted by a gunman in the old mineshaft. Thank God Jade had survived, unlike the poor girl that had been shot down there. Tammy Braithwaite, whose father was now in police custody. God knew what that meant for Brookhaven: one owner dead, the other facing jail. Ever since she'd found John's body, it felt as if she'd stumbled into some insane, alternate reality, a confusing and impossibly tangled web.

The doorbell rang again, and she gritted her teeth as she strode towards the main hallway. Who could it even be, at this hour? For a moment an urge gripped her to grab one of the kitchen knives from the locked cupboard under the sink. But there had already been too much savagery, too much damage done to human bodies and lives and reputations.

Seven dead in one night... and in quiet, boring Axton of all places. She could still barely believe it.

She rounded the corner, the stairs leading away to her left, the front entrance ahead. A man was waiting there, leaning forwards to peer through the glass. She froze.

Brian.

How could he be here? Her mind conjured the image of him in his gas mask, hidden amongst the trees. The dark orbs of his eyes seemed to reflect her sins back at her, judging her just as he'd judged his other victims. She cowered, almost crying out.

Then she realised it wasn't Brian at all. It was his likeness, superimposed like a camera filter onto a younger man, a man she'd met before. His son, the politician's assistant. Taking in a deep, steadying lungful of air, she strode towards the door.

'Owen, isn't it? How can I help you?'

Owen smiled, his breath misting in the dry, freezing air. 'Ahh, great. Stephanie. I'm really glad it's you. I need to talk to you. Can I come in?'

She frowned, sensing another interrogation. 'I... can't really talk right now...' she stammered.

'Please,' Owen said. 'I promise this won't take long. I need to tell you what my father told me before he died.'

She felt another shudder creep through her. *Another person who knew her business.* But surely Brian wouldn't have betrayed her confidence, even on his death bed? What would be the point? *To humiliate you, because that's what you deserve.* Her thoughts churned as she stood numbly aside.

'Thank you,' Owen said, rubbing his hands together to warm them as he stepped inside. 'I should have worn gloves. Look, I know this is going to sound crazy, but can you take me to John Harrington's office?'

She stared. She hadn't set foot in that room since she'd found John's body in there, the incident that had started this whole demented episode. Panic welled up suddenly inside her, a congealed knot that hung in her throat, making her feel short of breath.

'Why?' she gasped.

'I'll explain. You don't even have to come inside if you don't want to. Just tell me where it is. I hope I'm not too late. I should have come sooner, but it's been... a bad week.' He offered a friendly, forlorn smile, and her panic melted away as she felt a surge of sympathy for the poor man, a man who had lost his father in more ways than one.

'Follow me,' she forced herself to say, and led him towards the stairs.

'Everything all right, Steph?' called Marie, hovering suspiciously in the corridor.

Stephanie nodded. 'It's Brian's son, Owen. There's... something I need to talk to him about.'

Marie's eyes narrowed, and she watched as they ascended the staircase. She did not return Owen's smile.

'She looking after you, is she?' Owen asked as they reached the upper floor.

'I suppose so.'

'Just like you looked after my dad.' For some reason, the words felt like barbs. The acid sting of praise, undeserved. 'He was really fond of you, you know,' Owen continued, oblivious.

'That's why I'm here. Before he died, he said you and I were the only people he cared about.'

She led him along the corridor, hearing the echo of Brian's voice in the words repeated by this younger replication. Tears jabbed her eyes, and she said nothing.

'He said he wanted to make sure you were okay.'

They reached the door. She stopped a few paces before it, as though a huge, invisible hand was pushing against her, preventing her from coming any closer.

'He said that maybe something good might come of what he'd done.'

Confusion joined the maelstrom of emotions in her chest. All she could do was point at the door. 'It's there,' she managed.

Owen walked past her and stepped inside. She watched him through the open door as he glanced around a room he'd never entered, looking for something. It took him only a few moments to spot what he was searching for, and he approached the enormous painting. He wrestled with the huge canvas, eventually managing to remove it from the wall, leaning it against one of the nearby filing cabinets.

'So there really is a safe,' he said, half to himself. He glanced over his shoulder at her. 'Have the police been to check this?'

She shook her head. 'I don't think so.'

He nodded, and turned back towards it, removing a scrap of paper from his pocket. 'He made me write down a code for it,' he explained. 'He said that we should split the contents fifty–fifty.'

Slowly, he entered a series of digits into the keypad. The safe emitted a discordant beep, a little red LED flashing alongside the numbers.

'Maybe he was just babbling, from the painkillers they gave him,' said Owen. 'Oh, wait – that's a seven, not a one.'

He typed the number sequence again, more carefully. This time the tiny bulb turned green, and the safe's door cracked ajar.

'Or maybe not,' Brian's son murmured. His back was facing her as he pulled the safe open, so she couldn't see his expression, but somehow his body conveyed the widening of his eyes. 'Bloody hell,' he said excitedly as he reached inside, turning to show her what he'd found. There were stacks of money in his hands, more cash than she'd ever seen in her life. 'There must tens of thousands in here!'

Her mind whirled. She saw a road, forking unexpectedly. A new path.

Something good.

A new future for her, and for Nicky.

A way out.

She shook her head. 'You should keep it. He was your father, after all.'

But Owen was already counting out two piles of money on the desk, smiling sadly as he did so.

THE END

A NOTE FROM THE PUBLISHER

Thank you for reading this book. If you enjoyed it please do consider leaving a review on Amazon to help others find it too.

We hate typos. All of our books have been rigorously edited and proofread, but sometimes mistakes do slip through. If you have spotted a typo, please do let us know and we can get it amended within hours.

info@bloodhoundbooks.com